I Died

Seventh Blood

Author: Bree VanBibber

Chapter .... Page

Chapter 1 4

Chapter 2 25

Chapter 3 45

Chapter 4 66

Chapter 5 87

Chapter 6 105

Chapter 7 128

Chapter 8 148

Chapter 9 170

Chapter 10 194

Chapter 1

Heavy rain fell against the carriage window as Kenji leaned his head on the cool glass to relieve his fatigue. They had traveled this path a few times before as they approached the town of Hisley in the wee hours of the morning. This trip had been tiring however, as they had decided to bring the children along with them. It was in part to introduce them to Zax's family that resided in the secret forest of lesser dragons. The other reason was to meet with a certain goddess whom Kenji had a bone to pick.

Margret and Mara were taking their turn to watch over the kids, so Kenji had been trying to get some rest. The children, who were about two months old at this point, developed much faster than the average child. To the extent that all four of them could toddle and Darla was almost able to walk confidently. Regulus, Celenia and Titus weren't far behind, but their physical bodies were not quite as developed. They had all gained a basic understanding of language at this point. They were even able to communicate properly through telepathy.

While this did make caring for the children easier, it also meant Kenji's telepathic communication skill was almost always active. The children were also prone to complaining about how boring everything was. They did their best to keep them distracted with stories and by showing them the world passing outside the carriage. The children did their best to behave but they were still infants regardless of how fast they matured.

Zax, who had evolved into a Vampiric-Dragon Monarch after giving birth, was excited to show their family to the village. Dragons don't have offspring that often. In fact the last one born was Zax and that was a few hundred years ago. Thinking about that Kenji was sure the lesser dragons would hold a splendid celebration as they did for most big events. Kenji was just hoping they wouldn't get too wild.

"Papa?" Darla's voice rang in his head.

"Yes dear?" Kenji replied aloud to his daughter.

"Are we going to see grandma and grandpas'?" She asked with a sparkle in her eyes.

Darla was definitely her grandparents' jewel, and they had provided many play things for all the children since they were born. Toys ranging from dolls that Titus, Darla and Celenia liked, to wooden weapons that Regulus adored. They had been hesitant to give the fake weapons to the children at first, but with their quick development they were able to understand the importance of not hitting anyone with the wooden instruments. So far there had only been one injury to speak of, and that had been dealt to Margrets face in the middle of a tantrum.

The child responsible, Regulus, became inconsolable after the incident, blaming himself for hurting one of his mommies. But after some reassurance from Margret that she was ok, he slowly played more and more with the wooden sword. He almost seemed to be practicing so that he wouldn't hit anyone on accident again. Kenji wondered if the child would be a good fit for an instructor once he was grown. But all that aside they were nearly to the inn in Hisley.

Having the kids with them stretched the journey into about two weeks, but it had been a fun adventure. With Silver pulling the carriage they had also been completely safe from wandering monsters. All the same Kenji kept his sense presence skill at full power, and intended to do so until they were safely in Roxa's pocket dimension. There was no telling when Death, the giant skeletal dragon, would come after them again. Kenji was positive of one thing, he would keep his family safe.

Reid, who had volunteered to tag along, was also doing her best to keep the children entertained. She would summon light spells into her hands and show the dazzling light to the children. She kept doing this till Celenia, who was concentrating so hard it seemed like she might be going to the bathroom, summoned a light spell of her own into her tiny hands. At this point Reid lost it a bit at how a child could imitate a spell cast by a full fledged mage.

Once Celenia had a good figuring around the technique, she seemed to share her knowledge with the other kids. One after another, each child displayed the light spell they had been watching. Darla created a burst of light so bright that it temporarily blinded most of the carriage occupants. At this point Kenji instructed them not to use magic without permission, just to ensure they didn't get some random person caught in their spells.

The carriage slowly rolled into the town later that afternoon, and Kenji's detect presence spell alerted him to a familiar face. Rilgo, the guild master of Hisley, was waiting for them in front of the adventurers guild hall. The carriage came to a halt before Rilgo, but before he could handle whatever business they had with him, he had to get over the sight of Silver. The vamperic-hind looked at him and smiled to show that he was harmless.

But as the rows of sharp teeth reflected the sunlight the guild master nearly passed out.

It was decided by his right hand woman, Cadellia, that they would hold the meeting at a later time. She encouraged all of them to relax at the inn for a while until the guild master was back up to his regular standards. Kenji almost felt bad for the man, almost. But as they made their way to the inn for the evening Kenji spotted a new restaurant open off the main street. Suggesting they go there for dinner, everyone agreed and made their way over to the establishment known as the Filtered Hesnur, a bird-like creature that was known for eating berries that flavored its meat to be slightly sweet.

Kenji had only had the meat once before as the creatures were notoriously tricky to catch. As they entered, the sweet smell of the meat tickled everyone's senses and they excitedly took their seats at a table. While they were chatting idly a group of rough looking men walked in and sat at a table across from them. Kenji wasn't particularly worried about them, as they were still a fair bit weaker than his family. But he could sense they were all on the lower end of A-rank Adventurers. As he made this observation one of the biggest men turned and locked eyes with Kenji.

"Sizing up people should be done stealthily if you're not sure who's stronger." The mountain of a man said, taking a step closer to Kenji's group.

Suddenly there were four knives from the table being held at the man's throat. Kenji snapped his fingers as he stood from his seat, Margret, Mara Zax and Reid all pulling their blades away from the guy. Kenji moved quickly but silently to the man's side and grasped his hand. Giving it a firm and steady squeeze he smiled at the man as he let slip a bit of his energy.

"Woah there bud," The man said, holding up his free hand in surrender. "Wasn't looking for a fight, just some friendly advice. We were the ones probing your strength to begin with. Names Hammer, Rinden Hammer."

"Kenji," he replied. "We're here from the capital on business. What's a tough lot like yourself doing out here?"

"Hunting Mr. Kenji," Hammer said with a broad grin. "We got ourselves a full proof method for catching those nasty Hesnur that make their nests off in the third floor of the dungeon."

"Really?" Kenji said shifting gears as he was genuinely curious about the dungeon. "What kind of trick is it?"

"Well now, that there is a secret. Cant let the Kimple out of the bag or we could lose our job." Hammer said in a serious manner, but then leaned in closely to Kenji. "Got to get the right bait, see if you can figure it out from there."

"Very well," Kenji said, releasing his hand. "Thanks for the advice and happy hunting," he finished in a jovial tone.

The owner of the establishment came out at this time and took a look at the wares the adventurers had brought, paying a pretty penny for the lot of it. Then, apologizing for the wait, came over to take the group's order, five helpings of roasted Hesnur for the group, and they prepared dizzer fruit juice for the kids. It wasn't long before the staff brought out their meals and they all dug into the meat.

Kenji teared up thinking back to the roast chicken he had enjoyed so much in his past life. This meat was as close as you could get to that poultry flavor. He only wished that deep frying with breading would catch on in this world so he could enjoy fried chicken again. Renaldo was on the case, looking for something similar to the flower from Kenji's old world, as the grain used for bread in Rena had a nutty flavor that didn't pair well with the meat.

As they ate Kenji thought back to his old world, and thought about how so much had changed in the four years since he had arrived here in Rena. His tragic death in his old life having led him here where he functioned not just as a hero but the future ruler of Falist. Kenji still wasn't sure he was ready, but with the people he had to protect by his side, he was sure he could do just about anything.

They finished their meals and made their way towards the inn where a pale but fully conscious Rilgo sat in a chair waiting for them. Kenji teased the man for having gone limp at the sight of his pet. Rilgo ignored him and reached down into a bag that he had brought with him. Inside were the necessary documents for the group to enter the dungeon, though they would be whisked away to the realm of lesser dragons. Since the doorway into the dungeon was the access point for this hidden realm, the gang all needed their entry permits updated.

After this was complete Rilgo took the opportunity to try and suss out exactly what they were after this time, but a sharp look from Kenji shut him down. The guild master excused himself and the others gathered in their rooms for the night. A large room that Kenji and his spouses shared with the children and a smaller one for Reid. Kenji felt bad leaving her on her own, but it had the potential to get awkward should they invite her in with them.

Kenji was reassured by Reid that there was no need to worry, implying that she had seen enough of their lovey dovey interactions on the ride up. Kenji blushed a bit, but after giving her a playful punch in the arm they went their separate ways for the evening. Kenji was looking forward to having a real bed for the night, and crawled into it fully clothed while the others got the kids changed into sleep wear.

"You should really take your clothes off," Mara said as she sat down with Celenia in her arms.

"I'll get undressed in a bit," Kenji said defiantly, holding his hands out to take his daughter.

"Nuh-uh," Mara said, pulling the little girl away from her papa's arms. "You clean up first, then you can hold your child."

"Oh fine," Kenji said, jumping up from the bed, flinging his shirt into the corner of the room.

Kenji then got a towel from the night stand and produced a ball of hot water to soak the cloth. wiping the towel across his body, removing the sweat and dust from the journey. It wasn't until Kenji felt eyes burning into his back as he went to remove his pants that he stopped and looked around. His spouses all were looking in various random directions, but could do little to hide the blush on their faces. Zax hadn't even bothered to turn away as they let a little stream of smoke out the side of their mouth.

Kenji rolled his eyes, but couldn't help blushing a bit as he pulled his night pants out of his dimensional storage. The group hadn't had any alone time since the children were born, so he did understand how they felt. Still he was a little dismayed that they would direct their gazes at him like that. It was a little unnerving. Finished changing and cleaned off he returned to the bed so he could take Celenia from Mara.

"Now it's your turn," Kenji said with a smirk. "Don't worry, I'm polite so I won't stare at you like a hungry Hind-Luk."

Mara and Margret both got upset at this comment, and insisted on setting Kenji straight.

"I wasn't looking at you that way," Margret blurted out.

"I was." Mara said with a serious look on her face.

"Me too," Zax chimed in. "It's so impressive how cool you look doing anything."

"Zax?!" Margret called in astonishment.

"What?" Zax responded, crossing their arms.

"You were looking too," Mara said, fully betraying Margret's trust. "If you don't want to admit it, that's fine, but he is our husband so it is only natural to find him… alluring."

Kenji was about to die of embarrassment, and taking Celenia he walked over to the window to watch the sun set. He had become anxious at this time every day since Death had attacked them in the Capital. There was really no way to hide from his attacks, and he could be upon them in seconds. As Kenji's mind raced through the best plan of actions should the beast show up, a sparkle of light caught his attention.

Celenia had manifested the light spell that Reid had shown them in the carriage. Kenji thought about reprimanding her for using magic without permission, but her sparkling eyes told him she had done it on purpose.

"What is it, my sweet girl?" Kenji asked as he averted his gaze from the horizon.

"Papa," She began. "It's all ok."

Kenji realized at this point that his child was trying her best to comfort him, having sensed the negative emotions in his heart. He shook his head to clear his thoughts, and made a mental note to restrain his emotions a bit more when interacting with the kids. They were unusually perceptive of the group's emotional states. This was a good thing however because through empathy they were gaining the understanding of different emotions.

Kenji smiled down at Celenia and then walked back over to the bed as Mara and the others had finished changing. Kenji gave each of the kids a turn in his arms, trying his best to release a comforting aura for them. It worked well as they each took turns falling asleep in his arms, all except for Titus who was being fussy. Kenji walked around the room singing a little tune about a mighty prince who gave his all to his people so that they could all be happy. Another few minutes passed and Titus too was fast asleep.

Kenji laid him down on the mattress that had been placed on the inn floor for the children. Kenji was sure that cps would be called in his world but here it was simply the normal thing to do. He unfurled a blanket and covered the kids legs so they wouldn't get too cold at night. Kenji then made his way back towards the bed, but was stopped when a pair of hands gripped his own. Being pulled over to the two beds that had been pushed together somehow without him noticing. Mara pulled him into the bed and wrapped her arms around his waist.

"I've been wanting to hold you since we left on this trip." She said, batting her long eyelashes at him.

"No fair," Margret said, being careful not to wake the kids. "I want to hold onto him too."

Zax on the other hand didn't bother with lodging a complaint, and instead snuggled up between Kenji and Mara so their head was laying on Kenji's knee. Margret, seeming to give up on some sort of battle of pride, went to Kenji's other side and leaned against his shoulder. Kenji was happy to be there for his spouses but he was also dead tired. Deciding that he was going to sleep one way or another, he laid his head back and sank it into the pillows that were just a bit too soft.

It took a little while but soon Kenji was dreaming peacefully as the others stared at his sleeping face. It wasn't often Kenji let his guard down, and through lots of practice he could keep his detect presence skill up even in his sleep. They sensed how his mana radiated off of him as the skill continued to do its job. But they worried about him and if he could actually get the rest he needed while doing it. Looking down Mara saw the light scars that remained on his fingers from where two of his rings had exploded.

The main reason for this trip was a meeting with the Dragon god Roxa, first to seek her blessing on the children and second to plan out how to confront Death. While Kenji's spouses were sure that they could face him together, Kenji had serious misgivings about anyone other than himself fighting them. His experience in the battle a few months back had been fairly traumatic for him. Kenji was afraid of something after the fight, but whatever it was he was keeping quiet about it.

He wasn't foolish enough to think he was successfully hiding it, but he was also sure that his exact thoughts weren't going to be transmitted to the others. And although he had a good 'brave face,' they could all sense the slight trembling occurring in his heart. Not that any of them blamed him for being nervous, as a normal person hit with the dark energy Death could produce, would find themselves a pile of bones in seconds.

For this reason Kenji was also weighing out the option of turning all willing knights into his family so that they could at least survive the enemy's blow. A thought that previously he had been firmly against. This conflict was sure to end with the destruction of one of the forces involved. They all just had faith that Kenji would make it out alive. Even still they had their own individual worries about what would happen by this conflict's climax.

Hugging tight to their husband the group fell into deep sleep. The night passed quickly but it was a peaceful rest. The next day they gathered their supplies and put the children into their stroller for the trek to the dungeon entrance. They were given more than a few questioning looks as they advanced towards the doorway. While you could enter the dungeons first floor with family members, it was still weird to see literal babies taken in.

One of the guards went to say something, but Kenji simply raised his adventurer card and they stepped out of their way. Kenji's individual rank could no longer be measured by the guild, but that didn't mean they left him at a low level. He was Labeled as a class-V Adventurer, as were everyone in his family except the kids. Taking a brisk step through the doorway they found themselves in the dimensional pocket that held the village of lesser dragons. Waiting there for them was Zimmer, one of Zax's parents, and he bowed to honor their arrival.

The kids seeing him all reached out and whined as they watched him approach. Reaching into his robes he produced four delicious looking Dizzer fruit. Making a quick circle of the stroller he popped one into each of the kids mouths, where their fangs punched through and they began to drain the juice within. Zax laughed at how simply her father handled the kids, but was also simply happy to be home for a bit.

They slowly made their way down the path to the village, Kenji noticing several of the cave-like dwellings that seemed to be in use. Zimmer, noticing his drifting gaze, leaned over and explained what was happening in his ear. Kenji blushed furiously, but simply locked his attention straight ahead. They finally made their way to the village square, where most of the residents were waiting for their arrival.

That day they held a lavish party to introduce the children to Zax's extended family. They all fawned over the kids, but Darla with her dragon-like features made a big impression. Though none of the kids were left wanting for attention. Some of the lesser dragons did small spells to try and entertain them. The kids drank it in and began begging for permission to try the new spells they were seeing. Kenji figured there were few places safer for them to practice,so he gave them the go ahead.

Within twenty minutes, they were flinging water balls and flame spheres into the ceremonial fire pit at the center. The lesser dragons lost their minds over children that young using magic so nonchalantly. The party went on for the rest of the day and late into the evening. Once things finally calmed down the group went to Zax's parents' house and were presented with food and drinks galore to help them finish celebrating.

Kenji wanted to meet with Roxa as soon as possible, but he also understood the importance of spending time with his spouses' families. So they settled down for the night and did their best to sleep well for the next day's journey.

Chapter 2

Kenji and his group made their way to the temple that Roxa inhabited, coming across a surprising lack of beasts. It made it feel more like a haunted stroll than a trek through a dangerous forest. But Kenji kept his guard up the entire time just to make sure the kids stayed safe. But even The Reaper of the Young stayed far away from them. This disappointed Zax as they were hoping to get a chance at attacking it.

Mara however did her best to keep the group focussed on the path ahead, along with Reid who had some questions for Roxa about some of her spells. After just two days' journey they made it safely to Roxa's shrine. Kenji and the others walked through the hole that remained from their first visit to this place. On that occasion Mara had been unconscious, so this was going to be her first time meeting the spectral form of the goddess. She was equal parts excited and anxious knowing from Kenji's stories how capricious this being was.

As they made their way down the steps they couldn't help notice the insane number of books that had appeared. The dwelling place was filled to the brim with literature from every corner of the continent as well as a few from beyond. Much to their confusion, there was no sign of the Dragon god amongst the piles of reading materials. Kenji walked cautiously through the stacks in search of a sign as to where Roxa could be hiding.

Behind a pile of books located at the back of the shrine was an enormous four poster bed, easily big enough to house a dragon. Kenji grabbed hold of the side of the bed and lifted himself onto the top of the mattress. Their laying in the center of a circle of manuscripts was a middle aged and voluptuous woman. Kenji was quite confused as to who this person could be, but a light purple glow shimmering from their hair tipped him off.

"Roxa!" Kenji shouted, having gotten right in the person's face.

"Wahhhhhh!" The woman screamed as she sat bolt upright, connecting her forehead with Kenji's. "Ouch!"

Kenji stood back to his standing height and rubbed the bump on his forehead. The woman sat on her butt for a bit longer, seeming to have had the sense knocked out of her. Kenji seemed to have guessed correctly as to the identity of this person, her glowing purple eyes being a dead giveaway.

"Roxa, why do you look like this?" Kenji asked, reaching out a hand to help her up.

"Oh! It's you, Kenji?" Roxa said, accepting the gesture.

"Who else would I be?" Kenji retorted. "Now explain please. I brought my family along to meet you and here you are napping. Also… Could you do something about your attire?"

Roxa looked down at her admittedly disheveled appearance, her cleavage threatening to burst forth from the robe she was wearing. Giving kenji an oddly mischievous smile, she called out to the others.

"Oh my girlies and gents. Your boy Kenji seems to fancy my body. Whatever will you do to correct his...."

Kenji's hand gripped her head with enough strength to break the average human's skull. Roxa shouted in pain, tears rolling out the corner of her eyes, she was lifted to her feet and carried over to the edge of the bed. Her legs flailing frantically she tried to apologize but was met with Kenji's cold eyes. Making a high pitch noise as Kenji released her she fell to the ground in a heap.

Mara and the others had made their way over at this point and all seemed to have a slightly disappointed look on their faces. Even Zax who usually drooled over the Dragon god seemed disillusioned. Roxa lifted herself back to her feet, and with a flash of magic was dressed in a fine set of purple robes. Looking around as if none of the last seven minutes had happened, her eyes fell upon the strollers.

"Oh good…. There are more of you?" Roxa asked with a palpable tone of disinterest.

"And prey tell Roxa," Kenji said, landing behind her. "What do you find so unpleasant about my darling children?"

"Nothing, not a thing wrong in the world!!" Roxa stiffened. "What can I help you lot with today?"

"Don't get me wrong," Kenji exhaled exasperatedly. "We do have business with you, but why don't you explain your appearance first?"

"Silly me," Roxa replied, hitting her head gently with her fist and sticking out her tongue. "I guess you all probably don't know about homunculus, do you?"

"You mean those legendary artifacts that were brought about by the powers of alchemy?" Reid questioned.

"There is a Daughter of Sages for you!" Roxa exclaimed, clapping her hands together. "They were a failed experiment of sorts brought about during the war of the gods. Humans were desperately looking for a way to replenish their troops and protect innocent lives. Unfortunately, they were trying to step into the domain of the gods with their actions. So they were doomed to fail."

"So, being a god yourself, you decided to use their advancements to make yourself a new body?" Kenji asked, actually thoroughly interested in their answer.

"More or less, though I did make a number of improvements. Just increased the durability a bit so it will last for longer." Roxa commented, tapping her chin in thought.

"What's with all the books?" Margret asked, stepping carefully over a precariously stacked pile.

"I find in this form the act of holding and reading information feels more fulfilling than just summoning the info to my mind. Plus, it gave me something to do." Roxa said with a shrug.

Kenji tapped Roxa on the shoulder, and with a glance around at the others, pulled her along to meet the children. As disinterested as she had seemed at first, it turned out she was quite taken with the kids in a matter of seconds. Seeing their mana flowing around them she was quick to ask about their ability to use magic, and Kenji gave them permission to use the light spell they had learned. After showing off for a bit, Roxa became their self proclaimed doting guardian.

"Children with such talent are almost never born of the human race," Roxa pondered aloud. "I can't figure out if this is because you're all vampires or if it is something about Kenji as a summoned Hero. All that aside, what is up with this little angle?" she finished pointing at Darla.

"That's my daughter," Zax said proudly.

Roxa leaned back against the air behind her as she emitted enough magic to keep her from falling over. She summoned bracelets into her left hand and tossed one to each of Kenji's spouses, then one to him. They were golden set with purple mana stones, each one emanating a magical energy that left them feeling refreshed.

"A gift for the little ones." Roxa said cheerfully. "Go ahead and put them on their left hands."

Kenji walked to Regulus and slid the bracelet on his arm, by magic they adjusted to fit just right.

"Thank you," Mara said, giving Roxa a bow.

"No need to thank me," Roxa boasted, holding her head up in superiority. "It has some defensive magic on them, so they should stay safe in the face of almost anything. Other than that, I stored some spells in them that might prove useful as they get older."

"On that note," Kenji commented as he stood back up. "We need to talk about a few things."

"Of course we do," Roxa moaned, rolling her eyes. "Why would you ever stop by just to visit?"

"Maybe next time," Kenji continued, rubbing his eyes in frustration. "For now we need to talk about this." He finished holding up the hand that was missing two of the rings.

"I told you not to take those off," Roxa tried to reprimand Kenji, but the look on his face made her shut her mouth.

"And to be fair," Kenji retorted, "I didn't. They kind of exploded during battle."

"What on earth were you fighting?!" Roxa exclaimed. "I can't think of anything that would..." as her words trailed off a panicked look crossed her face.

"It called itself Death," Kenji recounted. "A giant skeletal dragon looking thing. It was truly massive and wielded terrifying power. Specifically the power to end life."

"No, no, no!" Roxa shouted as she pulled up some screens made of magic. Ancient text flooded across them as she frantically looked for some information.

Kenji wanted to stop her so he could get some answers, but his instincts told him to wait. Finally Roxa found whatever it was she was looking for and made a disgruntled face. Pacing back and forth for a moment she seemed deep in thought, then finally sank down to sit on some books. Looking at the group she held her words for a long moment, then began to speak.

"So remember how I said you have five years?" she asked, not meeting any of their eyes.

"Yes," Kenji remarked thinking back to their first encounter.

"Well, looks like I was off by about two years…" She continued now fully looking at the ground.

"You're a god aren't you?" Margret chimed in at this moment. "How could you be wrong about something like this?"

"That isn't important, what is is that we make sure Kenji grows stronger as soon as possible. What attacked you was a proto-form of the darkness. I don't know how strong it will become or how quickly it will gain its full power, but we need to beat it sooner rather than later. Otherwise…"

Kenji didn't like the way Roxa's voice trailed off. But taking a deep breath he calmed himself and walked over to her. Grabbing both her shoulders he pushed her back so she was looking straight up at his face. He was not smiling, but he also didn't seem to be angry.

"Roxa," he said in a clear voice. "What do I need to do?"

"Well," Roxa pondered for a moment. "I'd say we need to get you to the last two gods. Like Queli Jeshil they aren't exactly stationary targets, but there is a way to find one of them."

"Ok," Kenji nodded his head in understanding. "How do we find this god?"

"Go jump in a volcano," Roxa said chipperly, apparently happy that kenji wasn't mad at her.

Kenji kept his hands on her shoulders, but slowly began squeezing her as he had a dead pan smile on his face.

"Ouch!" she exclaimed. "Wait! I wasn't being dismissive, he lives in the network of magma tunnels that link all the volcanoes on the planet. It really is the best way to find him!!"

Kenji loosened his grip, but only a little.

"Ok, ok!" Roxa continued. "I can get you to the one he is closest to at the moment, his energy is hard to miss, so I can definitely get you to the right place."

Kenji sighed exasperatedly as he released her, and she began rubbing her shoulders to relieve some of the pain.

"You know," Roxa said as she stood and made some distance between her and Kenji. "You should be nicer to me. I've done a lot to help you."

"Yeah, yeah," Kenji nodded while his voice sounded very dismissive.

"What!?" Roxa shouted in indignation. "I brought you here, made you a vampire and made you the Hero of Falist, heck the whole world. Not to mention, look at all the stuff you've gotten out of it!"

"Did we just get called stuff?" Mara asked, looking over at Kenji with a questioning look.

"Good question," Kenji replied. "Did they?"

Roxa blanched as she seemed to look for a way out of the hole she had just dug, but seeming to come up with nothing, simply took off running. Kenji shook his head in dismay, but with a quick burst of speed caught up to and lifted Roxa by her waist. Dragging her back over where she was forced to apologize.

"Now," Kenji said with a full blown headache set in. "Take us to meet this god of… volcanoes?"

"Fire actually," Roxa said, kicking over a pile of books, a bad idea as a mountain's worth of literature collapsed on the far side of the shrine.

"Fine," Kenji continued. "Take us to the fire god."

"No way in the hundred levels of my labyrinth would I go with you…" Roxa began but hushed up pretty quickly when Kenji shot her a glare. "I really can't go!" Roxa went on.

"I'm far too fragile in this form to meet with him, plus he is kind of an ass."

"More so than you?" Reid asked, having remembered the question she had come with. "Also, help me out a bit with some of these translations." She continued making her spell book appear out of thin air.

"Yes, I mean no," Roxa said in a flustered voice. "He's just a very difficult being to interact with… you'll see when you meet him."

Kenji nodded, assuming everyone has someone they struggle to communicate with. But he was suddenly filled with dread at the prospect of meeting someone Roxa found difficult. Roxa did help Reid, albeit just a little, so she could keep translating her magic tome. Then she set to work preparing a magical portal to the location of the volcano where the fire god was currently dwelling.

The main thing left to decide was who all was going with Kenji to meet this god. His first thought was leaving Mara behind to watch the kids, that way if something happened they would be able to protect the children. Though with them being inside Roxa's pocket dimension they were about as safe as they could be. In the end it was decided Reid would stay to keep working on her translations. With Roxa's help she figured she could take care of the children for a few days.

With that settled Kenji, Mara, Margret, and Zax got their things together so they could embark on their quest. Roxa pulled a silver bell out of her pocket and gave it to Kenji.

"Ring this bell three times while passing magic through it and I'll open a portal back for you," Roxa explained as Kenji took the bell and added it to his backpack.

"Anything else we ought to know before continuing forward?" Mara asked as she laced up her boots.

"Lava will burn most of you alive," Roxa replied, tapping her chin. "So do be sure to use magic as you pass through his terrain. And don't egg him on any like you do with me, he will try to kill you if he gets angry. Probably a good thing you're meeting him now instead of earlier. I can't imagine you with his temper."

"Verry helpful," Kenji rolled his eyes at the dragon god. "I wasn't planning on being rude to him."

"Then why are you so rude to me?" Roxa blurted out in defiance.

"Cause," Kenji replied with a big toothy grin. "We're just close like that."

"Close huh?" Roxa repeated with a slightly bemused look.

Kenji nodded in affirmation as the portal Roxa had been working on solidified into a passageway. On the other side they could see a smoking volcano out on the open seas. Kenji cast cooling magic on the group and prepared to step through.

"Now behave kiddos!" Kenji called out to his children. "Be good for big sis Reid and Auntie Roxa."

Roxa tried to get in some snide comment of when she had agreed to be called an aunt. However, the smile on her face gave away the fact she was pretty excited about her new title. As the last of the party passed through the portal sputtered and began to fade out of existence. They were left standing on the beach of a volcanic island. Swallowing down any misgivings he had, Kenji motioned for the others to follow him.

Zax was sent out ahead to scout. As Mara and Margret used earth magic to make them a base to function out of. It took about thirty minutes for Zax to finish their trek circling the island. Kenji used his sense presence ability, but the island was completely uninhabited. In fact there was nothing out of the ordinary on this island besides the volcano.

"There's nothing here," Kenji said, looking around skeptically. "If Roxa teleported us to the wrong island…"

As kenji said this a deep rumble came from deep beneath the earth, collapsing the rock house they had constructed with mara and Margret inside. Kenji and Zax rushed to their aid, pulling off slabs of earth, trying to uncover their friends. Beneath the rubble they found a concave area, Mara had used a new skill of hers to stop the earth from crushing them. All the same it had scared Kenji more than he would like to admit.

"Are you sure there is nothing here?" Margret questioned as she dusted herself off.

"Not on the island," Kenji replied looking astounded. "It's below the island!"

As kenji directed his detect presence skill straight down he felt a wave of heat and anger hit him. It was like his mind thought his body was being burnt away, but then it stopped. A ring on his left hand cracking and falling off. Kenji understood the situation.

"Son of a Kitch," Kenji muttered. Then, he very casually began walking towards the volcano.

"What are we doing?" Mara asked jogging to catch up with Kenji's long legs.

"We aren't doing anything," Kenji said, emphasizing the word "we." "I need you and the others to make it to the water as soon as possible. I'm going to ruin this jerks day."

Mara faltered for a second, that didn't sound like her sweet kenji. Running forward she grabbed his arm and spun him around. There on his face was a look she had never seen before and hoped to never see again.

Chapter 3

Kenji kicked off the ground, his wings, which he hadn't used in a while, seemed to have gone through a transformation. They were more animalistic and bat-like, seeming to be made of flesh rather than magical energy. Giving them a flap he burst forward and up in a blur of speed. Coming to a stop in an instant as he reached the center of the caldera. Then, he positioned his hands out in front of him. Pulling them close to his chest with his palms facing down he began to gather his energy.

Margret ran up with Zax to where the stunned-looking Mara was standing. "What's wrong?" Margret asked.

"We need to move, now!" Mara said, making a mad dash for the water.

Margret and Zax exchanged worried looks, but knowing that Mara was probably correct, took off after her. Just as they reached the water,they heard a deep rumble coming from the direction of the volcano. Mara kept moving, however, taking off swimming into the open ocean. Zax and Margret continued following her as an intense pressure seemed to consume the island. Once they were a decent way out, they turned and were shocked by what they saw.

Kenji had gathered an insane amount of magical energy and was pressing it down on top of the volcano. It caused the mountain to shake and shudder as it was pressed downward. The island split in multiple directions as it became flattened by his power. Then, in a sudden movement of force, the island caved in on itself. Collapsing the magma chamber below. The crashing sound of rocks plummeting into the depths of Rena radiated outwards as the planet shook.

The waves out at sea becoming violent and crashing, but at the same time the others were being protected from the chaos with an impressive barrier. Mara was doing her best to hold up the spell, which she had only recently become able to use. Kenji continued to apply pressure to the ground below him, all but sinking the island into the sea. Then he suddenly lifted his hands and the crushing pressure stopped.

"What was that?" Zax asked as they made their way carefully back to an intact patch of island.

"No idea," Margret said, looking around in awe at the destruction that had been wrought. "Mara, did Kenji give you any clues about what he was planning?"

Mara swallowed hard, keeping her eyes locked on Kenji's back as he descended a few feet to better look at the damage he had caused. She was glad she had noticed something was off, but now what would she do about it? It wasn't like they could really take him on, at best, they could maybe incapacitate him if need be. Just as she was pondering this, however, the ground trembled beneath them. This time it wasn't Kenji's doing, though he was staring at what might be causing it.

Ripping its way through the ground and up onto the surface was a creature Kenji would have called a salamander. Flames billowed from the beast, as it burst onto the surface, the water rushing into the crater evaporating around its massive form. Steam continued to rise and as it did so magma boiled up from below to surround the creature. It looked up at Kenji with malice in its eyes.

"What gave you the bright idea of attacking a god?" The being hissed from below.

"What gave you the notion that hurting my beloveds was a good idea?" Kenji shot back, preparing an attack into his left hand.

The others put together at this point that Kenji had been enraged by this god they were to meet. It didn't explain away his violent method, but it did give them a reason. That ended up being enough to let them relax a bit as they were now sure he hadn't just gone rogue. All the same, there would be some strong words exchanged later, assuming they made it out alive.

"I'm a god, what care should i have if someone weaker than me is to fall?" The god cried out, whipping its tail on the ground in anger.

"Its the duty of the strong to protect the weak, what foolish redirect do you spout to say otherwise?" Kenji roared back as his ice spell completed. A large number of needle like ice spikes filling the air around the god.

"You wouldn't dare!" The beast yelled out as flames burst from every pore on its body.

Kenji moved his hand down and the spikes fell in towards the creature. The majority of the spikes fizzled into vapor as soon as they got close, but Kenji was expecting this. What his opponent hadn't noticed was the three or four larger spikes that he had held back until the area was filled with steam. Its vision now blocked, he drove down the last four spikes pinning the gods limbs to the ground.

"I see," the god spoke, looking at its surroundings. " To summon ice strong enough to touch my being. I was taking you too lightly..." the creature took a deep breath in, and directing his head straight down melted not only Kenji's ice but the rock beneath it as well. "My name is Stremlig, show me what it is you protect!"

Kenji had only a split second as Stremlig turned its head and sent a wave of molten lava towards the others. Without time for a complicated spell, he simply blasted Mara, Margret and Zax away with wind magic at close proximity. He was sure he'd hear hell about it later, but it got them to safety. Kenji only had a second to try and defend himself. The lava flowed over and around him as he did his best to stay conscious in the heat.

"There now," Stremlig chuckled, looking out at the water where the others had landed. "There is your mighty hero, burnt away to nothing in my magma prison. He died to protect you but now who will save the world?"

Mara did her best to hold a determined gleam in her eye, but inside she felt something crumbling. Margret looked on in stunned disbelief. Was Kenji really gone? She wondered. Zax on the other hand was starting to transform into their dragon form, a dark aura surrounding them. If this god had hurt their precious husband, they would not stop till this god was dead.

"Dont go killing me off." Kenji's voice rang out through the area.

"Impossible!" Stremlig cursed in an ancient language as it turned to confront kenji, who was standing , clothes singed and torn, but ultimately unharmed by the fiery magic of the Magma Prison.

"That was one of my favorite outfits," Kenji commented, discarding his tattered jacket. "Now why don't you try taking me seriously?"

"Impudent mortal," Stremlig roared as it gathered an alarming amount of magic into the air above it. "I'll kill you for sure this time!"

Blue flames engulfed the island as the god laughed maniacally. The heat was so intense that the others out at sea felt the water heat to an almost bath like temperature. Storm clouds began to condense above them as the heat and cold collided. The water fluctuating and the sky darkening, it seemed like this might be a hard fought battle. Then a darkness began to permeate the flame wall.

"Nice try," Kenji called out, flying forward towards Stremlig. His sword draped in black flames he made a swing at the god's head.

Stremlig bared its teeth and bit the sword's blade, and the gnashing between its massive molars and Kenji's steel made a horrendous noise. The two colors of flame pushing against each other it seemed like Kenji had the upper hand. But in the next moment his blade was broken into a thousand pieces. Stremlig let a superior expression cross its face but then found its head being crushed against the ground.

Kenji had spun around and landed a kick straight into the back of its head. Its skull hard as steel avoided cracking, but the impact shook its brain in its head. As it pressed into the ground cracks from the impact radiated out in all directions, with Kenji standing victorious on Stremlig's back. The god had completely lost consciousness with Kenji's last attack. Kenji used magic to restrain the god then made his way out to help his beloveds back into shore.

— — —

After around an hour Stremlig awoke violently. Finding that its body had been frozen in a large block of ice it began breathing fire in an attempt to melt its way out. Unfortunately for it, it had little to no effect on the restraints. Turning its head to the side it saw Kenji standing with the group behind him. Gathered round a fire drying their clothes. Kenji's eyes were closed as he seemed to be pondering something.

"Hey brat!" Stremlig called out, but Kenji ignored it. "Hey brat!" it repeated. "Dont ignore me! What in blazes have you done to me?"

"Restrained you," Kenji said without opening his eyes. "A precaution to keep you from launching large scale attacks."

"Dont give me that crap," It retorted. "No mortal can grasp the core of my mana."

"Agreed," Kenji confirmed without moving. "Your mana is quite complex, your temperament and actions seem to be fueled by said mana. I feel no qualms about having restrained you."

"Impudent creature," Stremlig cursed through gritted teeth. "What did you do to know that much about me? Did that blasted Dragon tell you?"

"Roxa?" Kenji asked, tilting his head to the side yet still refusing to open his eyes. "Very good guess, she probably did know but she definitely isn't the type to give out warning. And especially not to me," he added with a small chuckle.

"What's so gosh darn funny?!" Stremlig yelled its question, letting a stream of fire burst from its mouth towards them.

Kenji's eyes crept open as the attack approached and he snuffed out the flames with a swift movement of his sword's hilt. It was all he had left of his favorite blade, but it still served as a good focus for his mana. At that point Stremlig seemed both amazed and aghast at what it had just witnessed. This mortal was defusing its magic with some on the same wavelength. That should have been impossible.

"What in the name of the gods of old did you just do?!" Stremlig was enraged at this point, but curiosity had wormed its way into its voice.

Then, Stremlig saw it. Kenji's eyes which had been crimson now glowed with a mysterious power, looking like embers floating from a fire. There was a calm expression on his face, but he seemed to be holding something in. It was as though he was worried something might escape him if he weren't careful. Slowly a realization began to hit Stremlig. This punk wasn't imitating its power, he had somehow assimilated it.

"Figuring it out?" Kenji asked as he manipulated some flames into the form of a phoenix. "Quite the extraordinary power you hold. If I had met you sooner or been weaker then things might have ended differently. I might have gone mad even if you had let me take in your power willingly. Instead I took it while you slept, the bare minimum I could do to repay you for your attack."

"What nonsense is this? I don't know what that dragon told you but mortals cant have the powers of a god. It would tear your body apart, any mortal would fall into insanity as they were ripped limb from limb by the unimaginable levels of magic."

"I believe you, but I'm no simple mortal," Kenji said walking over to Stremlig. "I just so happen to be a Vampire, and a rather powerful one at that."

"I thought your kind went extinct?" Stremlig said, a look of horror crossing its face. "And even then it would still be destroying you."

"It is," Kenji confirmed, talking just loud enough that only Stremlig could hear him. "IT hurts and is trying its darndest to fight back against me. I assume it is because you yourself still wish to fight me, but I heal rather quickly. So while I'd like it if you were to change your mind, I can keep this going for the rest of my days if it lets me keep them safe," he finished gesturing with his head at the others.

"Youd go that far for another?" Stremlig asked, a different expression crossing its face.

"Forever and always," Kenji said, turning to look at his spouses.

A long silence passed as a gentle rainfall began, the storm clouds that had been gathered during their fight finally opening up.

"Let me go." Stremlig finally said in a hushed tone.

"Why would I do that? I can't guarantee you won't start fighting me again." Kenji commented nonchalantly as he caused his phoenix to keep the rain from reaching his beloveds.

"Because I swear on my core not to fight you any more." Stremlig replied in a somber voice.

"Ok," Kenji said leaning in closer, water flowing off his long hair that was falling into his face. "I'll let you go on one condition."

"And what would that be?" it replied looking at the boy, weary of what he might say next.

"Tell me where to find the Water god. Do that and we will have ourselves a deal." Kenji responded with a flash of lightning illuminating his face.

"I can't," Stremlig said, averting its eyes. "That would be impossible for me to do."

"And why is that?" Kenji pressed. He wasn't trying to threaten this god but it wasn't like he could just give up either. "Roxa seemed to think you would know where she was."

"Dont you dare lay a hand on her!" Stremlig said a new blast of heat radiating off of it.

"Why would I harm her?" Kenji asked. "I just need to get some of her blood."

"And I'm telling you not to taint her with your touch!" Stremlig roared.

Kenji held his hand up, and the heat wave dissipated. He felt like he wasn't really getting anywhere until Mara walked up beside him.

"May I speak to it for a second?" She asked with her usual happy smile at kenji.

He thought about refusing and sending her back over with the others, but as a wave of pain shot through his body he instead nodded and turned away. Mara smiled at his back, but then turned to meet the god's eyes. Her expression was cold, her eyes telling this god not to cause trouble. It reminded it of her.

Mara talked with the god for a bit, seeming to have cast some interference magic so no one else could hear them. The god's face changed to a number of expressions, but it seemed to stop being hostile. Whether that meant Mara was that scary or it was really being honest about not wanting to fight any more kenji wasnt sure. But the pain he had been feeling began to dissipate. About ten minutes passed as Mara continued her conversation, but suddenly she undid her interference spell.

"Good news," She said, walking over to kenji, setting her hand on his shoulder. "I know where the water god is, but she'll have moved somewhere else in the time it would take us to reach her."

"Great..." Kenji moaned, but seeing the look on her face he stopped himself. "Whats wrong?"

"The water god is very weak, compared to the other gods at least. Her life force is weaker than the others." Mara continued her explanation. "She relies on a group of devoted followers to keep her safe as she traverses the oceans of Rena. It might not be an exaggeration to say that taking her blood could cause her serious harm."

Kenji's face fell. "What would he do now?" He wondered. It was not like he could get the strength he needed any other way that he knew of, but he wouldn't risk killing someone just for power. He felt his heart beat in his ears as he searched his mind for a possible solution.

"Hey brat," Stremlig called out once more, though without any of the aggression it had used previously. "I know you have this big destiny you're supposed to rise up and face, but can't you do it without her?"

Kenji swallowed, not sure he trusted himself to speak. As he turned to look at Stremlig he felt a draining sensation engulf him. It was such an unmistakable feeling that he broke Stremlig free from his bindings more on instinct than on purpose. There in the sky, descending from the clouds was a dragon wrapped in black aura, and made of bones.

"Death" Kenji muttered as he took a half step back in genuine fear. "Everyone get back!" Kenji yelled as a beam of dark energy missed him by inches.

"What is that?" Stremlig called over as it scurried behind an outcropping of rock.

"That," Kenji responded, summoning a wall of stone for him and the others to take shelter behind. "That is Death, The one seeking to end all life in the world of Rena."

"Ha," Stremlig laughed as it poked out from its hiding place. "LEt me show you what my magic can do to a weak enemy like this."

As Stremling's body came into view it was hit dead on with a blast of the dark magic, knocking Strembling back and out from his cover. Kenji wanted to summon a new wall to protect it, but there was no time. Death began swooping around to their left to get aim at them. Kenji erected another barrier between them and death, but he knew their time was short.

"HEy brat!" Stremlig called out. Their body having turned a shade paler. "I got this, you guys just get out of here."

"No way," Kenji shouted back, repairing the barriers in front of them. "Even I won't leave a jerk like you here to die!"

Stremlig gave him something of a remorseful look, then turning its head shot a blast of fire in Death's direction. Kenji took this opportunity to rush to Stremlig's side and reached for his sword. Brandishing the hilt he was suddenly reminded that his sword had broken during his previous fight.

"I'm telling you brat, you and yours need to leave right now. You don't even have a proper weapon. You need to…" Stremlig was cut off as another bolt of dark energy missed it by a centimeter.

Kenji looked around, and finding a pool of magma, sunk what remained of his blade into the molten liquid. Concentrating mana into his sword he pulled out a cylinder with a jagged piece of volcanic glass protruding from it like the mighty blade of the scythe of the grim reaper. Brandishing it to his side a wave of fiery mana blast outward from his new weapon.

"Care to say anything about my weapon now?" Kenji questioned the god.

"Fine!" Stremlig roared as it fired another blast at death. "But if you all die, don't come crying to me."

"Back at ya," Kenji replied, readying his weapon to attack. "Now, follow me!"

Kenji took off with a barrage of flaming attacks flying all around him. This was not going to be an easy fight.

Chapter 4

Kenji's new weapon shimmered as he spun it, like the fang of a deadly serpent aiming for its prey. He was able to divert the attacks from Death as he flew towards it. The dragon had a smug look as Kenji closed the distance between them in a matter of seconds. Just as he came in range for an attack, the massive beast unveiled a new move, teleporting a few hundred feet away where it resumed its attacks on the island below.

"Where do you think you're going?" Kenji shouted as he too teleported over to the creature. "I'll be taking you down right here and now!"

As Kenji shouted this, his blade made a nice connection into the Dragon's tainted flesh. A burst of dark magic exploding from the point of impact. The energy was enough to wrinkle Kenji's hands, but not to injure him like taking a direct blast would have. Death turned as if to make a comment of his futility, but a flaming fire ball exploded in its face.

"Thy lineage be damned!" Death shouted as he focussed a beam of energy right for Stremlig.

Kenji was quick to rush to Stremlig's defence and spun his scythe so that it misdirected the beam off into the ocean. A bounty of sea life that had been minding its own business rising to the surface, rotting as it hit the air and any of the heavier pieces sinking back into the depths.

"Sure you want to keep fighting?" Kenji asked Stremlig over his shoulder.

"I'd worry about yourself," it replied, launching a pillar of flames up from the ocean and into the sky. It might have been a direct hit but Death managed to port away from the immediate danger.

"You call yourself a god?" Death's eerie voice filled the air around them. "The true gods were nothing as pathetic as you!"

As Death finished their taunt they appeared behind Stremlig, his mouth wide open for an attack of concentrated dark energy. Stremlig immediately shot a mouth full of lava into Death's maw, the two energies colliding and causing an explosion that shook the island. Waves radiated out from the force of the blast, and an injured death flapped its way up into the air again. Kenji went to chase after him but seeing Stremlig laying on its side, paused just long enough to sense if it was still breathing.

"Next time we meet," Death's voice echoed out again. "We will find out if you're truly strong enough to stand before me."

In a moment Kenji had zoomed up, his scythe shimmering in the light of the sun, he took a mighty swing and managed to slash Death's face. He let out a howl of anger, but in the next instant was gone from sight. Kenji spread his detect presence skill as far as he could, but not sensing the beast began his descent back to land.

— — —

As Kenji touched down he could see Margret, Mara and Zax gathered around Stremlig. The god was laying on its side, breathing heavily as it tried to keep its eyes open.

"You ok?" Kenji asked as he approached the others.

"We're fine," Mara replied, not taking her eyes off Stremlig. "But I'm not sure about it?"

"I'll live," Stremlig said in a pained huff. "Can't believe that thing is so powerful..."

"He's grown stronger since we last faced him," Kenji replied, keeping his sense presence skill active. "The way he is now I would have been a goner without..."

"...Without my power?" Stremlig said with a little pride seeping into its voice. "I see why you need our power now," it coughed as it finally sat back upright. "But I'm still begging you not to bring her into this."

"I don't understand," Kenji replied. "I was told I needed to feed on all of the gods to get the power to defeat him. Can't you see the threat it poses to the world of Rena?"

"Indeed I do," Stremlig replied, its eyes looking like centuries had been shaved off its life. "But there are other ways than following that damn dragon's plan."

"You mean Roxa?" Zax piped up in confusion.

"Yes," Stremlig continued, its voice cracking as it spoke. "The gods used to meet every so often, but a century or so back we had a falling out. Roxa wanted to have one of us serve as a sacrifice to hold the darkness back for a while longer, but we disagreed on who should pay the price."

"That's awful," Margret said, covering her mouth in abject horror.

"It was all but decided that my sister would play this role," Stremlig continued. "But I stood firmly against the plan as did Queli Jeshil who claimed that he could hold onto some of the darkness in exchange for some of our life forces. In the end we took his suggestion, but it affected my sister very negatively. Her body became slow and her energy became weak. She all but lost her godly status."

"And if I take her blood?" Kenji asked in reply, but already knew the answer.

"She will die," Mara replied in Stremlig's place.

"Exactly," it responded. "That was the heartless Roxa's true plan all along. My sister's death would indeed boost your power, maybe even beyond the realm of us base gods. Because in exchange you would receive her seed of divinity."

"Seed of divinity?" Kenji repeated. "I never heard anything about that."

"Because if you were the one summoned by the ritual we all chipped in to make," Stremlig said with triumph in its voice, "You would never willingly do it. Am I wrong?" it asked this time allowing a hint of a smile to cross its face.

"No," Kenji said, shaking his head. "Killing anything that wasn't trying to kill me was never an option."

"Good good," Stremlig continued, though its face looked tired. "I will help you, and so will my sister. So do me a favor young hero?"

"Anything," Kenji replied, placing his hand on its head. It was cold.

"Take this," it replied, closing its eyes.

Stremling's body began to harden like stone and cracks ran across its petrified form as the area around it became colder.

"No!" Kenji shouted, trying to force healing energy into the gods body, but there was no reaction.

"...Sorry Kid," Its voice echoed in their heads. "I was dead after the first attack that jerk landed… but dont worry… you'll be just fine…just dont… trust… Roxa…"

As Stremlig's voice faded like radio static Mara and Margret fell to their knees. Growing out of the gods body a beautiful tree emerged and bloomed, like flaming chery blossoms. There, hanging from a branch was an orb that seemed to be filled with stars.

"Kenji?" Mara said, wiping tears from her face as she looked up at him.

Kenji couldn't think of a name for what he was feeling and instead just allowed his magical energy to rush from within him. There was sadness and anger, appreciation and disgust. Had Roxa really planned to have him kill its sister for power? Was this small orb really so important?

Reaching out he grabbed the orb and gave it a gentle tug. Energy began to fill his being, not like feeding on gods in the past had, this was different. He felt his body breaking down and reforming very rapidly, and falling forward gripped his chest. This had to be a seed of divinity, and Stremlig had entrusted it to him. Just as the agony was about to consume him he felt three pairs of arms grip him tightly.

"You don't have to bear this alone," Mara said, one of her hands cradling the side of his head.

"LEt it all out," Margret added as another wave of magical energy threatened to blow them away.

"Whatever you decide, we're here for you my husband," Zax finished.

Kenji felt his mana stabilize slightly as a painful heart beat resonated through his body, like his chest was about to explode. Then the sphere turned into a trail of lights that went in through his nose with his next breath. A feeling like lightning running through his veins. The power was stronger than anything he had ever felt.

"You can do this," Margret cheered him on, though she was filled with anxiety, looking at the pained expression on his face.

Kenji tried to reign in his Mana, and doing so he felt the rest of the rings on his hands heat up and explode outwards. His beloveds catching some of the force of the explosion but holding firm to his frame. He suddenly felt his body become electrified, and sensing something dangerous coming he tried to get the others to let go of him.

"We're not going anywhere!" Zax shouted as a gust of wind enveloped the group.

"You have to get back," Kenji choked out as he tried to pull away more vigorously. "It's dangerous to be near me right now!"

Mara's hand slid into his own and she gave it a loving squeeze. "And we promised to be with you no matter what, right?"

Kenji looked at her, one of his Crimson eyes glowing white with energy. Her face showed no fear, just her ever present kindness. His brain begged him to get away from them but his heart was thankful they were so close. Then a bolt of lightning descended from the heavens and struck Kenji. In that moment time slowed almost to a stop. Kenji was filled with energy and at the same time everything inside him became unnervingly calm. The thrashing energy aligning within him as if it had found perfect harmony with the rhythm of his soul.

Just like that he had perfect control of all the power that was at his disposal. His spouses had been sent flying back by the electric current of the lightning, but as if time stopped he moved freely around the group. He grabbed Margret and Zax and rushed them to the side where they would be safe from harm. Then, turning back he lifted Mara into his arms and carried her to the same place. Setting her down he stood and took a deep breath. In a split second time resumed and there was an explosion where they had been standing moments before.

Kenji felt drained and slumped to the ground. His body felt light and heavy at the same time. A profound exhaustion and an equally unyielding energy both present in his aching body. Looking at the others who had all lost consciousness in the aftermath, he sighed slightly.

"You guys sure are a handful," HE said, quietly. Then, a smile curling the corners of his mouth, he continued, "but I wouldn't have it any other way.

— — —

About an hour later Zax woke up to find they were no longer on the island, and instead woke up inside what felt like their home. But it wasn't their home, not exactly at least. It actually reminded them a lot of the ocean side castle in Scelt where they had spent their honeymoon. But the air and energy was like what they knew from the Village of Lesser Dragons pocket dimension. The biggest difference to here was this sense of being surrounded by their beloved. Realizing they couldn't see him anywhere they went to wake up Mara and Margret who were still unconscious on the bed.

Once the group had risen and acknowledged their rather interesting surroundings they made their way up to a door. As they passed through it snapped closed behind them, and what had appeared to be a normal hallway stretched on for an eternity. On edge but not scared because they could sense Kenji's presence, they began to move forward. As they did so the walls on either side melted away, revealing moving pictures that had a young dark brown haired boy in it. They looked around, Mara and Zax hopelessly confused, but Margret saw it. He had the same eyes she knew from that first day he arrived.

"I think these are Kenji's memories?" Margret questioned aloud to the other two.

"Yes," Mara said, "His demeanor is no different to the one he has now."

"You guys think so?" Zax pondered, looking at a memory of kenji defending a young child from some ruffians, still being a child himself. "I guess he's just as brave as the one I know."

A wave of uplifting energy passed through them as the walls returned to normal and they found themselves at the far door. Looking at each other, they reached out in unison to push the doors open. As they did so an explosion of floral fragrance engulfed them. This room had walls that looked like blue skies and sprawling fields but the depictions moved in real time, with a gentle breeze rustling the grass. The room was filled with flowers.

In the middle was a high back chair with the back facing them. As they looked around at all the flowers they made their way to where they could see Kenji sitting in his chair. His right eye had turned silver, his skin looked like that of a porcelain doll and his hair was a magnificent Gold that shimmered in the light being omitted by the drawn sun behind them. They were all taken aback but the look on his face made them uneasy.

"Where are all these flowers from?" Mara asked a little hesitantly.

"Home," Kenji replied, his voice calm but full of emotion.

"What?" Margret and Zax asked in unison.

Keni rose from his chair and snapping his fingers a light blue portal appeared beside him. He looked at it longingly, and a tear came to his eye yet refused to fall. Then he turned to his spouses and pointed to the magical doorway.

"It leads back to my old world."

The others were stunned, but it lasted only for a moment. Then without exchanging glances or thoughts they all stepped forward and asked, "Can We Come With You!?"

Kenji looked at his spouses, and as the tear finally ran down his cheek he shook his head and said, "Nah!"

Kenji flipped his wrist to the side and the doorway shattered into trillions of shards that looked like fairy dust. Kenji looked around him with a warm smile the likes of which had never crossed his face in this world or his old one. He had wondered about popping over to get them some gifts, but he wouldn't risk not being able to return if something happened to him. 'No' he thought, 'I'm right where I belong.'

The others fell to their knees in exasperation as kenji took his seat in his chair, one that Mara recognized as being his favorite at the royal palace. Standing up she marched over and flicked her dear husband in the head. Kenji recoiled in genuine pain, but was definitely playing it up for her amusement.

"You know I'd never leave this world in peril, not with all your families still living here and in danger." Kenji said with his usual jolly laugh.

"Dont scare us like that, Margret said coming up and kicking his boot, which unfortunately hurt her more than him.

"Yeah," Zax said with maybe the most enthusiasm. "And I bet you're stronger now, so how about we have a duel?"

"No Zax," The others said in unison, but seeing their pouting face made Kenji laugh even harder.

"Listen guys," Kenji said with a twinkle literally emanating from his right eye. "One day I'll take you on vacation in my home world, but for now we have things that need to get done. Are you ready to get to work?

"Yes," they said together.

"Good, then first things first, what do we do about Roxa?" Kenji asked.

"What else?" Zax responded with confidence. "We just have to go kick her butt right?"

Kenji paused as if seriously contemplating the suggestion. Mara however grabbed both him and Zax by an ear and gave them a thorough talking too about not being too violent. Margret stayed quiet, though she did agree with Zax. After that was over Kenji conjured up some more chairs, and for bonus points a tray full of snacks.

"So what are we actually going to do?" Margret questioned as she was hounding her third hotdog. She thoroughly enjoyed the saltiness of the meat and the fluffiness of the bun. Loaded with chilli and cheese, she thought it was what heaven tasted like.

"Margret, your manners," Mara said, but having simply lifted her hand to hide her peanut butter fudge filled mouth. The texture, sweetness and creamy taste of the dessert had left her with childlike excitement over the new food.

Zax however was fully engrossed in their ice cream cone and was paying attention to nothing else. Wearing more of it than they got in their mouth.

"I say we test her," Kenji said, munching on some loaded fries, covered in melted nacho cheese, bacon, chives, and a huge glob of sour cream. He was also sipping some cream soda, a beverage from his childhood. Man had he missed carbonated beverages.

The table was overflowing with snacks and drinks from his old world. Via a simple summoning spell Kenji had brought over more delights for them to enjoy. Luckily the food being not native to the world of Rena made them taste normal to the group of vampires.

"What kind of test?" Mara asked, having swallowed her current mouth full.

"What if we see how she reacts to Strmlig's death," Kenji offered up. If she doesn't care that it died, then she probably wouldn't be bothered by its sister dying either. And depending on how she reacts to me we might be able to get her to admit it on her own. I'm not sure she's evil, but maybe she is thinking about all this the wrong way?"

"That's a fair point," Margret responded. "I doubt she would intentionally do something to harm another god."

"Unless she thought there was truly no other way," Mara continued. "What are the chances she properly listened to the other gods when they were pitching ideas?"

"Less than nothing," Kenji said, shaking his head. "She plays by her own rules, we all know that. Best case scenario we talk some sense into her."

"And worst case?" Zax piped up making a pained expression as they got brain freeze.

"Worst case we seal her up for a bit till we can figure out another way," Kenji said with a shrug. "As I am now I shouldn't have too much trouble taking her on."

"I guess we have our plan then?" Margret asked hesitantly.

"YEah, and I'll contact Reid just to be on the safe side, got to keep the kids out of trouble." Kenji said, licking off his thumb. "Next stop, the Temple of Roxa."

The others nodded in agreement, and as they stood to their feet they found themselves back on the beach. Kenji smiled at them, seeing how desperately they wanted to ask him about where they had just been. But giving them a quick telepathic message they all agreed to wait till later.

Kenji sent a thought out to Reid and after getting something of a confused response pulled out the bell and rang it thrice. A magical portal appeared before them, and with kenji giving them a reassuring nod, he headed in.

Chapter 5

As they stepped through they found their trip was a bit different on the return, they were suspended in the void, the magic within glowing and fluctuating. Kenji studied it for a moment before they popped out on the other side. They were set to follow through with their plan, but Roxa was throwing an unholy fit over the fact Reid wanted to lay the children down for a nap.

I'm telling you," Reid began as she pulled Regulus out of Roxa's grasp, "It's time for their nap."

"And I say there is no need for naps when they can hang out with their Favorite Aunt."

Watching the exchange Kenji had serious misgivings that Roxa had orchestrated such a nefarious plan. All the same, he signalled for the others to intervene and get the kids to a safe place.their arrival seemed to take Roxa by surprise, and the cold atmosphere pulled her back to reality.

"Whoa," She exclaimed turning her attention to kenji. "Youve powered up a lot considering Stremlig probably didn't want to cooperate. If I didn't know better, it looks like you've reached the level of a demigod. Did it give you some secret item or something?"

"You could say that," Kenji said, starting to walk so he was in between Roxa and the others. "I got a thing called a seed of Divinity."

"How did you get that?" Roxa said in stunned amazement. "That old coot gave up its godhood? I have a hard time imagining it doing that?"

"Well," Kenji began glancing at the others. "Stremlig is dead."

There was a long silence as Roxa tried to put the words she had just heard together in her mind. Then, there was a pause in her eyes as she seemed to contemplate her next words.

"Did you kill it?" She finally asked, no sadness or regret, simple curiosity seeming to be all that was coming from her.

"I did not," Kenji replied, tensing his muscles in anticipation. "Death caught it in its sights, attacked it and after being injured left it for dead."

The others didn't like how direct Kenji was being, but they knew this was for the best. If Roxa did have some hidden motivation, it was better that they know it now rather than later.

"I see," Roxa said, turning her attention to the sky as if searching for something.

"What are you doing Roxa?" Kenji asked getting ready to move in case she tried to run off.

"Then I suppose it told you about my plan?" Roxa replied softly.

"The one where I kill its sister?" Kenji questioned. "Yeah, it told me all about it."

Roxa looked down at him and smiled slightly. "Then you must know what an awful creature I am?"

Kenji was taken aback as Roxa released her soul from her humanoid form. She floated in the air and looked down at her talons. Gripping her claws a few times she extended her wings, but made no attempt to flee. Instead she bowed deeply to Kenji.

"I acknowledge my sins for being so careless with the life of another. I created this spiritual manifestation magic so that we could avoid all this ugly talk of killing and death. Life had to be lost in some form or another, but I would not have been satisfied with surrendering one of my own without a hope of bringing them back." Roxa stated as she turned to look Kenji in the eyes. "If you need to take your regret or your anger out on someone, please let it be me."

Kenji was floored at this point, the Roxa he knew was not so humble or apologetic. But he could see it. While there was no sadness there was real distress in her eyes. Kenji thought about his response for a moment, then took a deep breath.

"There are no such feelings inside me that need to be appeased. I simply wanted to know if you were capable of seeing a mistake." Kenji said in a clear tone.

"I'm a god, not a perfect being. Even the gods of old were known to admit their mistakes."

"Most gods I've heard of are supposedly infallible, but if you can admit to your faults that makes you better than the ones from my world. I see your sincerity Roxa, please return to your human form." Kenji said, taking a relieved sigh.

"What will you do with me then?" Roxa asked, a little reserved.

Kenji stood for a moment as he let his thoughts swim deep within his mind. He had no ill intentions, but if Roxa was willing to reflect on her actions and make a different plan, Kenji had an idea to help her out. Smiling to himself he looked up at the spectral dragon and made an offer.

"How about I keep you close for a while?" Kenji asked.

"What do you mean?" Roxa probed hesitantly.

"I mean you're going to come see what the outside world is like." Kenji continued. "With us as your guide we will show you the world you want to protect. If we can come up with a different plan we can find a way where no one else has to die."

"You sound naive for one who has stepped foot into the realm of the gods," Roxa replied feeling a little bewildered. "If I die out there then who is going to save the rest of my people?"

"I swear on my power that I can keep your people safe if you will let me?" Kenji responded. "I'm just asking you to trust me Roxa."

"Ha, I guess I've got no choice." She scoffed, but let a smile cross her maw. "I'll return to my vessel and prepare a few things. Then I hand my duties over to you. That's what you want right?"

"Exactly," Kenji said with confidence. "Starting today I will be the keeper of the dragons, and you will be the god Roxa, companion of the hero."

Roxa leaned forward and dove into the back of her homunculus, her soul squeezing its way inside. As her eyes fluttered open she was a bit shocked to see kenji holding out his hand to help her to her feet. Smiling, she took it and stood up. Then holding out her hand a purple sphere with pulsing blue energy inside appeared in it.

"Do I need to explain what to do with this?" Roxa asked.

"Nope," Kenji exclaimed, taking the orb and shrinking it with some of his divine power. Then he swallowed the ball.

"I admit that is a very practical way of taking in the core of this realm, but I really thought you might try something a little more scientific." Roxa commented, scratching her head.

"No need to be complicated about something like this," Kenji responded with a shrug.

"I take it we have reached an understanding?" Mara asked as she approached, Reid following close behind having successfully gotten the kids to sleep.

"What happened to you Kenji?" Reid asked, looking her friend over with that same curious excitement she got from studying magic.

"I'm a Vamperic Demi-god now," Kenji said, striking a silly pose to try and loosen up the atmosphere. The entire group laughed as he did a dance from one of the animes he used to watch in his old world.

"So I assume we're not fighting Roxa?" Zax questioned looking slightly disappointed.

"There is no need for any of us to fight." Kenji reassured them. "Roxa is going to be traveling with us for a while as long as the rest of you don't mind?"

The spouses exchanged looks then gave him an affirmative nod. They had all agreed they would follow his lead in this matter. But they did still feel a bit unnerved that they were going to be traveling with a god.

"You know," Reid said, feeling the tension. "In her homunculus Roxa is only about as strong as I am."

Margret let out a curse before quickly looking over to make sure none of the kids had heard her. Luckily they were all still asleep but that didn't stop Mara from grabbing her by the ear and giving her a talking to for cursing near the children.

Kenji laughed at his family, and slapping Roxa on the back gave her a nod to tell her to join the conversation.

"Now Lady Margret," She said a little tensely. "There are still plenty of things I can do with my diminished powers."

Margret looked at Roxa, a bit of complex emotions flooding her mind. "Just Margret is fine," she finally spoke. "Roxa, I have my own feelings about your plan, and while i dont think you are entirely wrong, I also deeply despise the part of myself that believes that. Can we trust you?"

Roxa was stunned to hear her thoughts, but looking at kenji, who was still smiling, she swallowed hard and responded. "I Know my mistakes and am aware of the harm I could have caused. But I promise on my divinity that I will never be the cause of harm to you."

"Very well," Margret said, holding out her hand. "Then, on my honor, I will do my best to keep you safe."

Roxa felt a new sensation as tears welled up in the corners of her eyes. She wasn't sure what this feeling was but she didn't hate it. Reaching out she gripped Margret's hand and gave it a firm squeeze.

"It's always cool when you show off your knightly side." Zax chimed in.

"Shut up Zax." Margret said, getting flushed.

Ried let out a small giggle as Mara put her hand on Kenji's shoulder.

"You're sure about this?" Mara asked telepathically so only Kenji could hear her. "I trust you, but do you trust her?"

"Not yet," Kenji replied. "But I want to try believing in her potential like she once did for me and you."

Mara felt the dragons core inside her pulse with energy as she thought about how Roxa had given up her mortal form for her. Then smiling walked over to engage with Roxa about how she would have to learn the rules for being in their kingdom and their party. Kenji smiled at the group, confident he could come up with a better way for all of them to get stronger.

Crossing his arms he began to wonder how the rest of Rena was holding up. Curious to see the outside world again he began ushering everybody to get their stuff ready to return to the town of Hisley. Roxa spent an eternity debating which books she would need with her and which she could leave behind. Kenji eventually told her she could only bring ten of them at a time, which Roxa was deeply distressed by. But kenji reasoned with her that as the core of the dimension was now his he could simply grab books for her whenever she needed.

Roxa gave up on her wish to bring all seven hundred with her in her dimensional storage, but relented when Kenji explained how impractical that was. They made their way to the entrance of the shrine, and everyone had their breath taken away by the lush green forest and bright blue sky that had filled the space. Kenji smiled as he walked over and grabbed an apple from one of the nearby trees.

"What about the Dizzer fruit?" Reid asked a little flustered that one of their main food sources had probably vanished."

"Dont worry," Kenji said tossing the fruit to Reid. "Try it and you'll see there is nothing to worry about.

Reid was confused but tentatively taking a bite felt her body flood with magical energy and renewed strength.

"What are these?" She asked, enjoying the sweetness of the fruit.

"In my world we call these apples, but the reason they work is because they are being produced by my Life essence." Kenji replied, handing apples to the others in the group.

"Wait," Roxa started in confusion as she too took a bite. "You mean you brought to life everything in my plane which was dead?"

"Not everything," Kenji corrected, pointing out the undead skeletal creatures that were hiding in the shade of the trees. "NEed to keep your shrine safe in case you ever feel the need to return."

Roxa was slightly taken aback. Had kenji always spared this much thought towards her?

"What's up?" Kenji asked as Roxa's face flushed a bit.

"Oh, nothing!" she responded feeling her heart race as she seemed to realize that there were a lot of things she still had to learn about the mortal beings. And this man that stood in both worlds was probably the only one that could show her.

Smiling to herself she felt excitement begin to stir within her. When was the last time she had felt so exhilarated about her existence? But calming herself she followed the group towards the lesser dragon's village.

Within a few hours they were greeted by the very confused villagers as well as Zax's parents. With Roxa's help they were able to explain the difference in the dimension as having to do with Kenji's taking ownership of the realm. Galfix and Zimmer were delighted that their son in law had become more powerful, and Shral was almost overwhelmed by emotions as she got to meet the deity of her people.

After a little time talking it was evident that Zax's family really wanted them to stay an extra night, but knowing the knights were waiting for them Kenji politely turned them down. If they didn't get to Hisley today the knights accompanying them would be leaving without them until receiving a message from Wendy, Feni or Jennie that the group had returned. Keeping in mind the fact the kingdom was short on knights, Kenji convinced them of their need to head out.

The villagers gathered and waved goodbye as Kenji opened a gate to the outside world. Roxa looked at him surprised as that should have been her original magic. But looking at Kenji she smiled and figured there were probably a lot of things he could do now as a demi-god. With the thought of how fun it would be to teach him her magic, she felt a smile cross her face.

Doing her best to hide the expression the group passed through the portal back into the outskirts of Hisley. They made their way to the town and Kenji waved down one of the escorting knights to let them know they would be traveling with an extra person. He was saluted after Mara walked up to confirm that it was Kenji who was addressing him.

The rest of the time they were in town kenji kept to his room with his spouses so that his appearance wouldn't raise too many questions for Rilgo to have to answer. In all honesty he felt like a lot had happened to him in such a short span of time.

"Kenji?" Mara asked as he sighed.

"Do you think I'm doing the right thing?" Kenji asked.

"You mean about trusting Roxa?" Mara asked, a little confused.

"No, not just that." Kenji mused "Is it right for me to become something inhuman again?"

Mara saw what he meant, he had lost a lot becoming a vampire all those years ago. But this time was different and she was going to show him that. Calling over Margret and Zax they all gathered around him and gave him a big hug.

"Whatever you choose, whatever you become, we've got you." Mara said looking deep into his eyes.

"Yeah, " Zax said, leaning in and giving him a kiss on the cheek.

"No matter what, you're our Kenji." Margret agreed with the other two, brushing her hand down Kenji's back.

"Right," Kenji confirmed, a more confident look filling his eyes. "Then tomorrow lets start doing our best to find another way to save this world."

"Agreed," the others said in unison.

Just then a knight came and called for the group to prepare for departure. IT had been a busy couple of days, but Kenji felt sure they could find a way forward as long as they were together. Smiling, he stood up and gestured for the others to follow him. And of course they obliged, as would till the end of time.

Chapter 6

After a quick discussion over how they should address Roxa in front of others, they landed on calling her Roxy. It wasn't that they thought many people would realize her godly status, but they wanted to be safe rather than sorry. Kenji introduced her to the knights as a powerful mage that they had befriended on their travels. Several of the knights that had been with Kenji's group on previous adventures, exchanged looks that said they weren't buying it. But as a testament to Kenji's strength they snapped to attention as he cleared his throat.

"Roxy will be staying with my party for the foreseeable future, so I expect all of you to show her the proper respect. I consider her something of a mentor, and will not tolerate anyone challenging her." Kenji continued his speech to the knights. "And I'm sure some of you have questions about my appearance, but you need to keep in mind that there are some things you don't need to know before the king does."

The knights snapped to attention and gave Kenji a salute before setting to their tasks so the group could depart. Kenji took a deep breath and rubbed the bridge of his nose. There was so much that he was going to have to explain to the king, and he wasn't sure where he would start. But he also had the other issue which was the knights chatting in what they thought were hushed tones about if Kenji had found another bride to take in.

Luckily, Mara's stern glare was enough to snap them back to their work. Kenji didn't particularly care what the others thought, but he was not happy being pictured as some kind of maniac trying to marry every person that caught his fancy. All the same the more people misunderstood Roxa's true identity, the happier Roxy would be. The point of her coming with them was, in no uncertain terms, to show her the beauty of a world she hadn't seen in centuries.

"Roxy," Kenji called over to the seemingly normal young woman. "Please stay out of the knights' way as they handle their tasks. We don't want to hold any of them up with your curiosity."

"Right, ok," Roxy said as she stopped attempting to climb to the top of one of the carriages. "I just wanted to get a better look at the area."

"I know," Kenji said, placing his hand on her head. Then, leaning in, "You might be able to get a better view if you just ask."

Roxy looked confused, but as Kenji extended his wings from his back he held his hand out to her. She looked a little nervous, but accepted the invitation. Kenji lifted her into his arms and flapped his wings in a single mighty burst. They shot up a few hundred feet into the air in a matter of seconds, then he spread his wings wide and glided around the outer gate of the town.

Roxy looked like a kid who had just been given candy for the first time. Her eyes twinkling in the light of the afternoon sun. As she looked out her eyes glowed slightly as she used magic to increase her vision. Kenji flapped a few times to move them in a wide circle, allowing her to get a view of the entire town of Hisley. After a few minutes she seemed excited still, but otherwise satisfied with her time up in the air.

"Been a while since you flew under the open sky?" Kenji asked with a slight smirk on his face.

"No less than a thousand years ago," Roxy commented, not looking at him as she spoke. "Ever since I built that dungeon, I've been hidden away."

"Are you nervous?" Kenji asked as she seemed to shake a bit in his arms.

"Wouldnt you be?" Roxy returned the question.

"I was," Kenji said with a sad chuckle. "For me this was a whole new world, a whole new life. Your spell brought me here, and I was worried what I could do in a place like this."

"I guess I owe you an apology?" Roxy said in something of a somber voice. "My apologies for pulling you into all this..."

Kenji shushed her as she tried to continue. "I don't feel like you owe me anything of the sort. You gave me a new life, and I was able to find my family here. I just hope you can find something to protect."

"Kenji..." Roxy began, but seeing the look in his eyes she quieted herself, then in a meek voice said something where most people couldn't hear. But, Kenji had pretty good hearing and with a small chuckle replied. "Your Welcome Roxy."

About that time Mara sent Kenji a message that they were almost ready to go. So flapping gently he flew back over to the carriages and touched down next to his beloveds and Reid, their kids having already been loaded in. Kenji helped the others get loaded as well, then walked over to ride on Silver's back for the first leg of the trip home.

— — —

The trip was, for the most part, uneventful but they did have fun explaining some of the changes that had occurred in the region as of late. Much like Zax, Roxy found even mundane things like how magic stones were used in farming quite interesting. The best thing and main difference was she never demanded to have the carriage pull over so she could go look. But that didn't mean they didn't stop to show her things in more depth.

The trip was mostly uneventful, with the knights guarding them they never had to lift a hand. That said, they did get out and fight when monsters appeared, it just meant that the knights had gotten strong enough that they would have been fine without them intervening. It was mostly kenji who fought, still getting used to his vastly different powers now that he was a demigod. While all his spells and abilities worked in basically the same way, he had to tone down how much power he put behind them. Compared to his old self he was letting out ten times the energy.

Kenji even had to refrain from using his absolute presence ability as it seemed to be affecting the knights in a negative way. The weight he exuded was enough to bring the men and women guarding them to their knees if he exerted even half his strength. Kenji didn't mind though, as he was still excited to see what he could do with his divine power. Another change he noticed was with his Eye of Jeshil. He could see and process an abundant amount of information around him as he fought. Things like the tensing of muscles as enemies went for attacks, the shivers as they tried to retreat and most importantly: how tainted by darkness his foes were.

The levels of darkness even in weak creatures seemed to be increasing at a frightful rate. But none of them seemed to be evolving or directly influenced by their tainted forms. Instead they were just more ferocious as a result. As Kenji finished clearing a pack of Kon Heizers, Wolf like creatures that breathed fire, he took a deep breath and refocussed his energy into the center of his being. Maintaining his power at all times was a challenge, but he was doing his best to master it before he was confronted by anything stronger.

He was far too aware that he was still a fledgling in the realm of gods, and as such was vulnerable to attacks. He was grateful that he also healed much faster without needing to rely on blood anymore, but as he focussed energy into a scratch he had sustained during the fight, he was also aware of how much his new abilities took out of him.

Roxy assured him that with time and practice his vessel would catch up to his power. The next step would be challenging the variants that she was sure had appeared during their absence. Things like Goblin Kings were just the beginning, as Roxy listed off other unknown creatures that she remembered from the War of the Gods, when she herself was but a fledgling deity. But as fearsome as some of the creatures sounded, she gave no hint that they would be of a particular challenge to Kenji as he was now.

All the same, Kenji couldn't be everywhere at the same time. They figured they would need to come up with a plan to minimize the amount of time it took him to traverse the kingdom so he could conserve his strength. The other problem being how villages on the kingdom's outskirts could relay their plight without risking the lives of adventurers unnecessarily. Roxy and Kenji talked at length about the plans to combat the spreading darkness, but decided to keep from making any big decisions without the presence of King Ridol.

As they drew closer to the Capital of the Kingdom, Roxy seemed to get a little nervous for her first in person meeting with the king. Kenji assured her that Ridol was a kind man who, while eccentric at times but, usually kept a level head.

— — —

Kenji had been honest, and believed his words in the carriage had been truthful. However, as Ridol was currently being helped off the floor where he had fainted hearing

Roxy's true identity, he felt a little concerned. The man's eyes had definitely taken on some age since Kenji had first met him. There was an air around him that Kenji could sense in his heightened form. The King was old, and had lived a full life, but he was still a mortal man.

Kenji seriously questioned if he was ready to take over the duties of a King, but also deeply wished Ridol could retire sooner than later. Kenji viewed the man like a Father, and really wished him a long and happy life. In a previous meeting he had even offered to turn him and Jasper, so the two friends could live on, but was met with thankful yet firm refusals. They both wished to one day rejoin their loved ones in the flow of nature.

Kenji had to stop himself at that time, as he wanted to argue for reasons they should turn, but the honesty in their eyes when they told him their wish to be reunited with their loved ones, he couldn't. All the same Ridol still had some fuel in the tank as kenji checked the level of darkness present in his body, only sitting at about half. The man might be aging, but he still had a soul burning with fire.

Ridol, as if reading his mind, gave Kenji a warm smile. "I'm fine my dear son," he began. "I can handle the throne for a bit longer, but I so look forward to the day you take your place upon it."

Kenji returned the smile and continued introductions to Roxy. Kenji left out stuff he didn't think was important, but said she was going to be staying with him as they thought up a strategy to defeat Death. While Ridol still seemed rattled by her presence, he understood the reason behind it. Cautiously he extended his hand towards Roxy.

"I thank you for aiding the Hero and our kingdom," He began as Roxy returned the gesture. "I truly hope you find a way to help Kenji save our world."

"Of course," Roxy replied. "Thank you for having me. I can honestly say I've never seen a kingdom thrive like yours has. You must be an outstanding ruler."

Ridol did his best to keep his composure, but the compliment had definitely struck a chord in his heart. His body relaxed a little and he offered up his kind smile. Seeming to do his best to keep tears from falling, he cleared his throat and motioned for them to all take a seat. Jasper went to prepare drinks, but Kenji stopped him, pulling several glass bottles of cream soda from his dimensional storage. While he had access to his old world, he had stocked up on some of his favorite things.

Ridol took the bottle, and after being assured it was not alcohol, followed Kenji's example and twisted off the top. It made a light popping noise and hissed as the carbonation leaked out. Jasper, who had also taken a bottle when offered, was the first to sip the beverage. His eyes flying wide open and sparkling with excitement, he urged the king to quickly take a taste. Ridol was also surprised by the rich creamy flavor that tickled his nose as he swallowed.

After insisting that they be made aware of how to make the mysterious drink, Kenji assured them he had plenty to share and would not charge them for what they were praising as a delicacy. He also brought out baked cheese snacks and passed them around. Roxy had already tried both of these items during the trip to the capital, but was more than happy to munch away at them as they continued their discussion late into the evening.

— — —

Roxy and Kenji made their way down the cobble street towards Kenji's estate, the spouses and kids having been escorted home earlier in the evening. Roxy kept looking around at the closed stores and bustling pubs. Kenji offered to let her go inside one of the establishments, assuring her it had the best kebabs in town. Hesitantly she agreed and they made their way to a back corner table. As soon as they sat down however, a small girl with dirty blonde hair and pigtails came up to them.

"Evening, Mr. Kenji?" Harper questioned with a mischievous smile. "You look different?"

Kenji smiled at the young girl, and seeing his fangs she seemed to be reassured this was the Mr. Kenji that she knew. "Hello Harper, Good evening." Kenji said just to make sure she realized it was actually him.

"Hungry for Papa's cooking tonight were you?" she laughed the question, but leaned in real close for her next one. "Do your partners know you brought some big boobed lady out to eat with ya?"

"I'm so sorry, dear hero. That is you right?" A large man with rippling muscles asked as he pushed his daughters head down. "And apologies to you too miss," He continued doing his best not to look at her bosom.

"It's Fine Rory," Kenji said with a laugh. "And yes Harper, my spouses know she is with me. She's a friend who will be staying with us for a while."

"Does that mean she's also a monster?" Harper tried to ask more but Rory shoved her off towards the kitchen with instructions to fetch Kenji and his guest their drinks for the evening.

"Sorry again Sir Kenji," Rory said in a sheepish manner. "I know you're not the sort to get mad over my daughter but I still feel like she has some more learning that needs to be done.

"Like I said," Kenji said, gripping the man's shoulder in a reassuring fashion. "No need to fret over it, we're friends aren't we?"

Rory blushed a bit as he straightened his apron. "Indeed sir, if that is your wish then I gladly consider you a friend."

"Good, good," Kenji chuckled. "Then friend of mine, can we get 30 kebabs to go? Feel like feeding the family a treat tonight."

"Cooked rarely I presume?" Rory asked, putting back on his usual business smile as he jotted down the order on a piece of parchment.

"That would be great Rory," Kenji said, flashing a smile. "Tell your wife that we would be happy to have you all over for tea sometime soon. I got my hands on some rare delicacies that you might be interested in trying to recreate."

Rory's eyes lit up a bit as he thought about foods that the hero personally vouched for. Assuring Kenji they would find a time that worked for them to come visit, he made his way back to the kitchen to get their order ready.

"Roxy?" Kenji asked, seeing her face, her eyes seeming to have gone out of focus as if she had been dazed.

"Oh sorry," she said, straightening up in her seat. "I was just pleased to see that those around you are still willing to accept you as you are now. I'll be honest it had crossed my mind that the further you got away from the mortal realm the harder life might be for you."

Kenji was shaken a bit to hear that Roxy had been concerned about such a thing.

He was still trying to wrap his head around what kind of being she was, but hadn't really stopped to think about what he was becoming himself. He glanced down at his porcelain white skin, a lock of his golden hair falling in front of his left eye. He was something different now, but he felt the same.

"What exactly does it mean to become a god?" Kenji asked in a quiet tone.

"It means you have more power than you think," Roxy began, seeming to choose her words carefully. "Helping others, or in fact hurting them becomes a matter of will. The simple whims of a god have the ability to affect the many one holds dear."

"But isn't that true for all power?" Kenji questioned.

"You're not wrong," Roxy replied, looking at her hands. "Power and strength are inherently able to change the world around you, but what you'll gain is a more absolute strength. Defying death is but a small part of what you will be able to achieve Kenji. But..." Roxy paused for a second.

"But what?" Kenji pushed gently, wanting to hear her true thoughts on the matter.

"But it's not my place to tell you how to use your strength, nor is it the place of any other being, living or dead," Roxy continued. "You will have to make your own choices in your own time. And Kenji, not all of them will be the right choices..." As she let her voice trail off she seemed to be contemplating her own choices that had led her to where she was now.

"Roxy?" Kenji called out to her softly.

"Am I a monster Kenji?" She asked in a hushed tone.

Kenji thought about her question for a few long moments. She seemed to be seriously reflecting on her question, but kenji wasn't sure how to reply. Then, as if the words came to him from somewhere else entirely, he whispered his reply.

"Do you feel like you're a monster?"

"I don't know," Roxy said, her voice trembling a bit as she looked up to meet Kenji's glowing eyes. "But… But I don't want to be one."

Kenji smiled at her then snapping his fingers time seemed to slow to a crawl around them. Then he stood from his seat and walked over to Roxy. placing his hands on either side of her head, he held it steady so their eyes met fully.

"My eyes have grown pretty special, I can see a lot more than you'd think." Kenji began as he stared deep into her. "I can see the methods behind magic, the meaning behind spells, and to a certain extent the desires of the soul within. Do you want to know what I see when I look at you?" HE asked.

Roxy felt an insane amount of magical pressure surrounding them. From what she could tell Kenji had made a pocket of temporal interference centered around them. They were cut off from the rest of the world. No one would hear his words but her. She swallowed as she looked back at him.

"Tell me Kenji," She spoke in a shuttering voice. "What is it you see? What am I?"

"Youre a silly little girl trying to live like you've put it all together," Kenji said letting a soft smile cross his face. "You've lived for so long without allowing yourself to experience what it is to have a life. You've acknowledged your power yet hide away from a world that seems so fragile. And Roxy," he continued, "You're not wrong."

"Im not?" She asked in surprise.

"No," Kenji pressed on. "With the powers beings like us possess, we really do have to be careful. But we are living creatures, which means we will make mistakes. You can't live in fear of that though, you have to be willing to fix the wrongs you create. That's what I see in you Roxy. The ability to right your own wrongs."

Roxy felt a welling of emotion fill her chest, but she didn't cry. Instead she gave kenji an affirmative nod, showing she understood his words. Kenji sat back down, and snapping his fingers again they returned to the natural flow of time. As Roxy glanced around in a mixture of curiosity and amazement, Harper came up to them with a big paper bag.

"HEre you go Mr Kenji," she said, then turning to Roxy she extended her hand. "And nice to meet you too, Miss…"

"Roxy." Roxy replied. "And it's been a pleasure to meet you as well my child."

Harper seemed a little confused, but giving Roxy a toothy grin she ran back to help her parents.

"If you think I can become a good person, I'll try my best," She said as they stepped out of the pub.

"That's all I ask of you," Kenji spoke as he turned towards his home. "And remember, If you need help I'll be here for you. You're not alone Roxy."

"I see," she said looking up into the night sky as they walked.

"Are you ok?" HE asked as they turned towards the front gate of his estate.

"I am," She said with a renewed sense of confidence. "If you believe I can do it, it seems foolish to dwell on my past mistakes."

"Very good," Kenji said in a hearty voice. "Then this is your first lesson." he continued pushing open the front door. His spouses waiting in the entry hall for their arrival, and the children already laid to rest for the night.

"What lesson is that?" Roxy asked, confused.

"Welcome home!" The other three exclaimed.

"Glad to be home," Kenji replied, then looked at Roxy. "Go on, you too"

"Glad to be…" Roxy began as she felt a warm emotion filling her heart. "Home?" she finished in a question unsure of what it was she was feeling.

The group of vampires smiled at her, and for the first time in a long time, she felt like she belonged.

Chapter 7

About a week had passed since their return to the Capital, and Roxy spent about half that time locked away in the estates basement trying to come up with a plan. She did stop for the occasional snack or conversation that was brought to her by Mara, Margret and Zax. She also took plenty of time playing with Titus, Darla, Regulus and Celinia. Between Kenji's children and the local kids who stopped by from time to time, Roxy had embraced a very motherly attitude towards them all.

During the night she slept like a proverbial rock, and little could wake her from her deep slumber. They had settled on pinching her cheek with some vampiric strength to force her to rise in the mornings. But as the routine fell into place, she seemed quite happy with where she was staying and what she was doing. It wasn't until another mostly peaceful week passed, that kenji had her stop strategizing for a day to accompany them up to the guild. While they had received documentation representing Roxy, they still needed to go through the signup process through the central guild.

As they made their way over, Roxy was yammering nervously about how she wasn't sure she was fit to be an adventurer. However, when Kenji asked if she intended to just live off their finances, she quickly straightened up and agreed to the registration process. She was a proud being, all be it one who enjoyed an afternoon nap in the sun with a good book. As they entered the Guild hall people were rushing around, but only looking a little stressed rather than panicked.

"Need to see Karjel," Kenji said, walking up to a fairly new receptionist.

"What?" he said looking up at Kenji with a confused and maybe somewhat scared expression. "You don't mean the guild Master do you?"

"That is who I'm referring to," Kenji said with a little laugh. "If he is busy we can wait for a bit."

"Um no, I mean…" the man seemed deeply confused about what to say, but finally spit out, "He's tending to the recent monster outbreak coming from the east."

"Oh?" Kenji said in surprise. "Has his majesty been informed?"

"The King?!" the receptionist said, almost passing out. "I don't know for sure, but it isn't the place of adventurers to bring up the royal family so lightly."

"I take it you don't recognize my husband?" Mara said, stepping forth.

"Crown princess Mara!?" The man blanched as he tried to stand to a salute, but in the process poured his morning cup of what kenji would have called coffee all over his pants. "I'm so sorry!" He continued as he danced around a little in pain. "That means you must be…?"

"Sir Kenji," Karjel's voice rang out loudly, causing much of the rushing to pause for a second. "Now aint you become something grandiose? How can we serve you today my lord?"

"Simple sign up for our newest party member," Kenji replied to the man with a warm smile.

The Dwarven man scratched his head as he looked at the group, and finally landing his eyes on the unfamiliar face of Roxy, turned a shade of red that had nothing to do with his temper. In fact there seemed to be an odd thing happening with Roxy's face as well, as she had averted her eyes so quickly from Karjel's it seemed she had pulled something. Kenji looked back and forth, and deciding now was not a good time to mess with the two, he made a move to signal they should go to Karjel's office.

"R...Right," Karjel stammered but obviously doing his best to pay attention to Kenji. "We can go up and take care of your... your party member here..." His voice trailed off a bit, but then he suddenly seemed to regain his composure as he continued. "To be honest we're in a spot of trouble if you guys wouldn't mind helping."

"Of course we will if we can," Zax spoke up. "But umm... what snacks do you have?"

Karjel who was thankfully used to Zax's bottomless pit of a stomach, cracked a small smile as he instructed one of the bustling guild staff to bring some fried higgle meat to his office. Once they had made their way up to his office, he led them inside and they all took seats. Karjel seemed to still be distracted so Kenji took the opportunity to start the conversation.

"We're here for miss Roxy's registration, but I understand there is some trouble that we may need to take care of first?"

"Oh, uh yes." Karjel said, straightening his back as he looked down at a map of the area. "We have reports flooding in of a hoard of monsters coming this way from the eastern forests. They number about four hundred from what my scouts reported back, they are still in the open plains so now is our chance to attack. That being said, we are waiting for a message from the King to approve mobilizing the knights to protect the capital."

"Meaning we need some adventurers to clean up the monsters?" Kenji questioned. "Would you like us to take care of it?"

"I mean, if you would like to take charge I can gather all the available…" Karjel began.

"No need for that, Our newest recruit needs to stretch her wings a bit." Kenji interjected.

"This lass?" Karjel questioned giving Roxy a quick glance. "No offense to her or you sir Kenji, but is that a good idea?"

"It will be fine Karjel," Kenji continued. She isn't a vampire like us, but she's got plenty of fire power at her disposal. And for certain reasons I'd prefer not to get the other adventurers caught in the cross fire."

"Well be that as it may, I still have to follow procedures, even for your party Sir Kenji." Karjel said, pulling at the tip of his beard.

"How about you accompany us then?" Mara asked. "Treat this like a ranking test and see for yourself the strength of Roxy here."

"I mean," Karjel responded, scratching his head. "If that is what the crown princess requests of me I can't very well say no."

"Trust me," Kenji said with something of a bemused grin. "You'll be swept off your feet by the time we are done.

Karjel looked like he wanted to make a comment of his own, but looking between the group members around him seemed to think better of it. Instead he shook his head and turned to retrieve his battle axe from behind his desk. If he was going with these youngins he was at least going to take care of protecting himself. No way would he just sit back and observe.

— — —

That is what Karjel thought, but as the group teleported over to the east side of the capital, the horde of monsters sent a chill down his spine. There weren't any strong variants or A rank monsters, but most of them were b rank with what seemed to be an army of c rank creatures under their command. Just as he was about to take his battle stance however, Kenji signalled for him to hold back.

"Roxy," Kenji said, looking over the fields. "I don't sense any living creatures near the monsters. Go ahead and be a bit flashy with your spells."

"A mage?" Karjel said, looking at her in surprise. "I would have lost money if I were betting. I thought you were a priestess of some kind."

Roxy looked both happy and embarrassed by Karjel's words, but seeing Kenji's serious expression decided she better step up and do her best.

Karjel watched in a mixture of amazement and confusion as Roxy started reciting her spell in the draconic tongue. He was just versed enough in ancient and forgotten languages to pick out the word 'fire' in the middle of the chant. Then, a wall of flames sprung from the ground, encircling the monsters and stopping them in their tracks.

"By the gods of old," Karjel breathed the curse under his breath.

"Roxy," Kenji asked, shaking his arms to loosen up his joints. "How long can you maintain this spell?"

"Fifteen minutes as long as I don't have to expand the range any," Roxy replied with a confident smirk.

"That will have to do," Kenji replied, looking around for a good place to leap forward from. "I'll take the big guy."

"What big guy?" KArjel asked looking around, but then he saw it. Crawling from the deep forest was a huge skeletal giant. The kind of creature put in children's fables to make them obey. An S rank monster.

"Kenji," Karjel said with a panicked expression. "Tell me you have a plan."

"Of course," Kenji commented over his shoulder. Then getting down low to the ground his new wings, which were still bat-like but radiated a pale white glow, extended out behind him. "I'm going to hit it really hard."

Before Karjel could comment on Kenji's so-called plan, the vampire was gone from sight. Flying at an incredible speed, he cocked back his fist and sunk it into the skeletal giant's sternum. It reared back and roared in agony as cracks spread across its breastbones. IT was hurt but not down.

Mara tapped Karjel who still looked quite worried at the situation, and gave him a quick smile before starting a brisk walk towards the captured enemies within the wall of flames. Karjel thought he should stop her, but as Margret, Zax and Reid began strolling up with the same nonchalant attitude, he felt his sense of reason falter.

Mara took the lead, summoning draconic magic of her own to summon two gleaming blueish-purple blades from thin air. Her first chance to use the weapons Kenji had provided for her. They ignited in black flames as she slowly picked up her pace until she was running full sprint at the center line.

Margret pulled a great sword from her dimensional storage that Kenji had taught her to manipulate. The sword was about as tall as she was, and curved like a katana. She pulled the blade back with seeming ease as she lined up for her first strike. Taking on the left flank with every intention of showing off her new skills.

Zax Summoned up two gauntlets from their own dimensional storage skill, which Kenji had also taught them. Slamming the gauntlets together fist to fist, they did a roll of their shoulders to loosen themselves up. Letting out a roar backed with Draconic magic, the enemies to the right focussed their attention on them.

Reid was the last to take her position, calling forth the magical tome but only using it as a form of arcane focus, as she had memorized most of the spells within. Chanting almost fluently in the forgotten tongue which Roxy had been helping her to learn, she called forth what Kenji had called a meteor to strike the back line.

As the forces of monsters began to scatter the other three set off to deal their own damage. Margret was quick as lightning, wielding her massive sword in a way a young prodigy might handle a wooden sword. Attack after attack, slicing through the enemies before her. In less than a minute she had dispatched about half her foes.

Zax, not wanting to be shown up, reigned down punches as they ripped through the enemies before them. The varied shrieks and shouts of the monsters like music to their carnage. About the time they had managed to take out roughly a third of the minions, they leapt high into the air and smashed their fists into the ground causing a shockwave to radiate out and feeling a good number of monsters.

Karjel let out some stammered words of amazement as he walked next to Roxy. "By the light of dawn, they seem more like monsters than the enemy."

"Oh yes, quite the monsters indeed," Roxy said with a small chuckle. "These young ones could give the gods of old a good fight I imagine."

"Surely you jest," Karjel began, but looking at Roxy's face he felt a nervous energy fill his gut. Those eyes were not the eyes of a young girl, and they radiated a power that made him believe her.

Then, there was the sound of screams and splattering blood as Mara ripped her way through the center line. The back group having mostly been decimated by Reid's spell, she was making sure she got in her kills. Her blades gleamed as they sliced through foe after foe, as if it were a warm knife through butter. Lightning spilling off the blades as she went.

After five minutes of clashing and carnage, the battlefield fell mostly quiet, the flaming wall still standing just in case. The other vampires regrouped with Roxy and Karjel, taking deep breaths to recenter their minds and recuperate their energy. Karjel was so amazed by everything he had just seen, that he almost fell over. But there was still one fight going on.

Kenji was throwing punch after punch into the skeletal giant's body, and as more and more cracks appeared across its form the more the beast tried to stop the inevitable. It thrashed around violently trying to catch up with Kenji's speed, but he simply was too fast for the creature. In all honesty Kenji might have been able to beat it with a single punch, but was using the enemy as an opportunity to learn how to control his strength with greater precision.

Seeing that the others had finished however, he leapt back a few hundred yards and braced his feet. Kicking off one more time he allowed that warm life energy to flow through him as he sank his fist into the monster's chest one more time. The being glowed from every crack he had made and it exploded into a million pieces, reigning down over what had become the barren battlefield. As the giant's remaining pieces turned to dust, Kenji spotted and caught its massive mana core.

The magic crystal from a beast like this was probably destined to be put into the royal family's care, but as future king he had an experiment he hoped Ridol would let him perform with the jewel. Walking back over with the boulder sized core on his shoulders, he set it down just to the side of the group.

Walking up to Karjel, he wiped the sweat from his brow and patted the dwarven man on the shoulder. "Looks like we've wrapped stuff up here," He said jovially. Think we can get Roxy an appropriate rank after her display?"

"Blast it boy," Karjel replied as he patted the man on the back. "I'll give her my job if you ask me. You folks just keep getting stronger, and I've never seen magic used on that scale before."

"I'm afraid that's the best I can do for now," Roxy chimed in, mostly to Kenji. "This form makes it harder to manipulate my mana."

"You mean," Karjel spoke hesitantly. "Youre not human either right?"

Roxy blushed a bit as she realized she had let slip her secret in front of someone outside the group, but Kenji gave her a reassuring nod.

"Karjel," Kenji began. "We can't tell you all the details, not yet at least, but Roxy is the oldest one here by far, and if she released her full power it could easily change the map of the continent."

Karjel swallowed hard, and mostly by accident, mumbled aloud, "To think I was feeling smitten about being so powerful?"

Roxy, who had been putting out her flames tensed suddenly and the remaining fire exploded into showers of sparks. Kenji did his best not to laugh at them, watching as Roxy turned to reprimand the guild master for teasing a maiden's heart. Unfortunately this only set him up to defend himself by retorting how love had no manners. The two went back and forth for a time, until they both seemed satisfied with an agreement that they were attracted to each other, although both had concerns about the age gap.

The group made their way back on foot to the guild hall, none of the vampires in the group willing to get in the way of the blooming love between the two. By the time they had reached the guild, Karjel had mustered up enough courage to ask Roxy to accompany him on a trip to town in the near future. Roxy, still being somewhat bewildered by "this young one," relented to the proposal. The group had many things to work on in the upcoming month, and they were still working on a plan to beat Death. All the same Kenji and his beloveds encouraged them to have a good time.

As Karjel dipped into the guild he gave a wave to the group. Kenji had been given permission to take the mana gem to the castle on his own, as transporting it through the city without his dimensional storage would potentially cause a panic. So the group made their way to the royal palace.

Ridol was excited to see them as he always was, but upon seeing the monster's core for himself, turned a little pale.

"That came from a beast this close to the capital city?" He asked with a nervous tension creeping into his voice. "But you all are fine, yes?"

"Never better father," Mara replied, giving her dad a small hug.

The color returned to his face, but he still radiated a nervous energy. He had questions about where the hoard had come from and what they could do to stop such incidents in the future. At the mention of his concerns, Kenji brought up his idea for a use for the magic stone.

"A barrier?" Roxy and Ridol asked in unison.

"Yeah, magic that keeps certain things out of a specific area, does that type of magic not exist?" Kenji asked in confusion, sure he had seen something like it in a remote village.

"It has been theorized," Reid chimed in. "Unfortunately no one has pulled it off. That is except for the ancient relics like the old shrines of Roxa poses."

And even I don't know exactly how those work," Roxy admitted. "They were another byproduct of the war of the gods that I just pumped some mana into."

"Then let me take a crack at it," Kenji responded with a mischievous smile.

After a long discussion about how and where they would establish the barrier, Kenji was escorted to the tallest spire of the Palace. Placing the monster core in the center of the watchtower's guard post, Kenji placed both his hands on the spherical object's surface. Pushing his will within with a single thought in mind, "protect the people of Falist.

Magical energy pulsated and glowed from the mana gem inside the core. And as the unusable parts faded away and the inner jewel finished crystalizing, an explosion of energy radiated out in every direction. It made no sound and did no damage however, as a force field expanded out and covered the entire castle and continued out to the inner walls of the city. It didn't reach everywhere he wanted, but at least this made a safe area for the townspeople to be able to evacuate to.

Roxy commented on how impressed she was by his ability to pull off the utilization of an original magic, and Ridol thanked him repeatedly for his hard work and dedication to the people of his kingdom. Kenji just wished he could do more.

Chapter 8

After establishing the main barrier, Ridol posed a question that kicked off an entirely new venture for Kenji. His simple musings on if Kenji could create smaller less powerful barriers out of lower ranking mana stones breathed fresh air into their situation. While Kenji wasn't sure that a weaker stone could handle the job for a long term solution, if it would allow a village to hold out long enough for help to arrive that was good enough. The biggest problem would be procuring the magic stones needed.

Luckily, about this time Karjel made his way in for a meeting with the King and Kenji about the clean up of the monster hoard that had been wiped out by Kenji's family. The number of beasts having been somewhere in the hundreds, approaching a thousand. About a third of them were Class B monsters, whose stones would work more than necessary for their plans if everything went smoothly.

The trick would be installing a mechanism to control the activation of the barrier, and with a quick port over to the now abandoned village of Shimal, Kenji took a look at the shrine with the ancient mechanism. Surprisingly, it was just a simple matter of plugging in a catalyst to ignite the mana and cause the spell to complete. The ancient device was so damaged though, it was a miracle it had worked in the previous disaster. It was no wonder Roxy couldn't reverse engineer it in its current state. Kenji was really only able to thanks to his upgraded eyes.

Having his answers, he ported back to where Roxy, Reid and Ridol were waiting. Karjel, having returned to change the delivery of the magic stones from the guild storehouse straight to Kenji's residence. Ridol began making plans to have knights deliver the completed devices to the villages across the kingdom, but Kenji had misgivings on letting someone else install them. If he was going to trust these devices to work across the continent, he felt he should place them himself.

He also reasoned the more villages he visited personally the easier it would be for him to respond to disasters. Instead of traveling by carriage or flight, he could simply port to any place that needed him. Ridol pointed out the urgency with which the dispersion of the devices should be conducted, and they compromised. Kenji would set out on a journey to every village he had missed on previous trips across the nation to check the installations, but the initial setup would be done by the knights of the kingdom. Kenji wanted to argue that a mistake in setting up the barriers could cost them the lives of people, but Ridol dropped a big point on him.

"As a king there will always be people you can't save," Ridol said with a stern tone. "If you can't trust your people to do at least some of the work, you'll never know a moment of peace. Besides," he continued with a serious look. "I would prefer you spend some more time with your family."

Kenji wanted to argue, but he knew Ridol was right. He just wanted to make sure no one died needlessly, however, the reality was he couldn't save everyone with his power alone. While it was a hard pill to swallow he agreed to let the knights handle the distribution in favor of spending time with his family. Roxy assured him she would help make the devices idiot-proof. Slightly reassured by the god's offer to aid him, Kenji backed down from his initial plan.

After starting a mountain of paperwork that Ridol and his council would need to get the knights mobilized en masse, Kenji and Roxy were set free to go begin creating the devices. They stopped by the modest tavern and inn run by Rory, Harper's father, and her mother Marcele. Ever since Roxy and Kenji's heart to heart a week previous, they had been frequenting the shop. Roxy was in love with their meat skewers and Kenji didn't mind saving some effort for their chef Rinaldo Trisk.

While the man had a burning passion for cooking, Kenji was worried he had too much on his hands with the ten occupants of the house. Kenji had offered to take in more staff, but Rinaldo insisted he would need to train them from scratch. So Kenji had given him leave to do so. Ridol had offered to let him pick his trainees from the castle staff. But Kenji and Rinaldo had declined in favor of creating new positions to be filled by some of the town's folk.

Rory had shown interest in the position, but Kenji told him that if he stopped running the inn it would make him and the others very sad. The food he made, always on the rare side, for Kenji's family was one of their favorite treats. Plus, taking him from the town's commoner inn felt like it would cause problems for many people. As a means of reassurance, Kenji had promised Rory that should hard times ever fall on them, he would do his best to support their business. Rory thanked Kenji for his gracious offer, but prayed to himself that those days would never come.

— — —

With Sir Kenji's Backing he felt he was on top of the world. As Rory packed up their order he remembered that his meeting with the young man was scheduled for the following day. Sir Kenji was going to be showing him some unique foods for him to try and recreate. As Sir Kenji took his parcel of food, he was kind enough to offer Rory a word of reminder about their appointment.

Rory watched as Sir Kenji and the Monster girl headed through the door and out to the street. He was glad that the so-called Monster Hero had grown into such a splendid young King to be. He had no time to waste however as the night crowd came in for the changing of shifts for the knights. Another gift from Sir Kenji, as before his arrival to the world of Rena the inn never hosted the knights due to its low born status.

Rory rolled up his sleeves and got back to work, but the rest of the night his mind was clouded by what Sir Kenji could offer for him to try and recreate. The excitement and nervous energy was driving him crazy, but as his wife's hand clasped his own, he was brought back to reality. It was the early hours of the morning, and his hands were wrinkled from having absently done dishes since they put out the fire.

"Rory dear," Marcele called to him in a gentle voice. "That man's got a gentle soul. Don't be worried about messing something up. He'll surely guide you forward should you ask."

Rory looked at his wife, a mixture of gratitude and acceptance. He was sure she was right. Even if he were to make some lapse of etiquette or not make a dish to meet his expectations, Sir Kenji was a good man. He had no reason to think he was a danger to anyone, but Rory felt this sense of foreboding any time that girl was around. All that aside, he would probably be meeting with Sir Kenji in a one on one setting, or at least that's what he expected.

At the mansion estate that belonged to Kenji, Rory bore witness to a scene straight from a fairy tale. There in Sir Kenji's front yard was a legendary beast. A Hind Luk at first glance but obviously something was mixed into it. Before Rory could calm his heart about that issue an upstairs window burst open. Flying out the window was what appeared to be a tiny dragon, about the size of a Kitch, gliding backwards towards the Hind Luk.

Rory's parental instincts kicked in and he flung himself to catch the baby dragon before it could be attacked by the Hind Luk. Grabbing the child he fell to the side and skidded to a halt right next to the beast. The creature turned its attention to Rory, and seeing him holding the baby dragon, bared its teeth. All to shout, "Mighty fine catch young lad!" in his face. Rory did surprisingly well by not passing out, but Sir Kenji coming out to save him at that moment felt like a blessing from the gods of old.

Sir Kenji laughed a bit as he took the baby dragon from Rory's arms and offered him a hand to his feet. The Hind Luk that Sir Kenji called Silver, leaning over to ask if he was ok. It seemed the color had drained from his face as a result of his previous moments of terror. Rory, seeing as he wasn't in imminent threat of being eaten, brushed down his hair and tried to recenter himself.

"Mighty interesting to see you raising a baby dragon, Sir Kenji." Rory began a conversation in hopes of getting things back on track.

"Oh, I guess you've never seen her do this," Sir Kenji replied. "This little one here is Baby Darla. You know her mother is a dragon right?"

"I see," Rory said, scratching his head for a second, then leaning forward he got a better look at the baby dragon. Its scales were the exact same color as the ones he had seen on Darla on her memorable first stop by his inn.

"Also, Please feel free to drop the formalities. Kenji is just fine on its own."

"Right," Rory said a little sheepishly. "Then Kenji, May I ask what you have brought me here today for?"

"Of course," Kenji said with a little bit of a bow.

Rory followed behind Kenji as he was led into the 'Haunted Manor' that Some of his old adventuring buddies had warned him was a cursed property. Rory discarded these silly roomers to the side of his mind as he focussed on making sure his feet were clean enough to walk on the interior carpets of the entry hall. After making sure he was good he glanced up to see Kenji handing the child, who seemed to have reverted to her humanoid shape to one of Kenji's spouses. Princess and Queen to be, Mara Thertis Mutori.

Rory didn't know why but the thought of seeing her in her home felt very different than when she stopped by the inn to talk with his wife. But, as she met his eyes and gave him a warm and inviting smile he felt himself relax a bit.

"Lady Mara," Rory started. "It is a fine pleasure to see you in good health today."

"Our home is your home Dear Rory, Please don't mind me and this playful child of mine."

Rory didn't know what to do in the face of such warmth and amenability from someone he perceived far above their station. But as the child in her arms began to sneeze he swore he saw the spell formula for a fireball form in front of its mouth. That is it would have formed had a tissue not been shoved in the infant's face. The high pitch sneeze muffled by the cloth and a small puff of smoke leaking from the infant's nose.

"This is why you shouldn't go outside on your own, Darla," Mara said, magically cleaning the tissue and using a second spell to repair the singed cloth. "You start sneezing and causing a mess."

Rory laughed nervously, as Kenji leaned over and poked Darla on the cheek.

"Yep," Kenji said with a smile. "Those allergies of yours will get you in trouble one of these days. Now then," he continued turning towards Rory, "Let me show you to our Kitchen. I have a friend waiting excitedly to see if you can recreate her favorite treat.

Rory followed behind Kenji as they made their way back to the main kitchen, and to his dismay he saw the young monster girl sitting on a counter waiting for them. On the outside she seemed like your average young noble lady, but that didn't stop his senses from warning him of the danger she posed. He really had no idea what it was about her that set him off, but the air of danger was unmistakable.

"This is Roxy," Kenji began with a gesture at the girl. "Youve met in passing but I'm not sure I ever gave you a proper introduction."

Rory nodded, and against his better judgement extended his hand to the young woman. Roxy accepted the gesture and gave a firm shake all the while keeping a sweet smile on her face. It was like she was peering into his soul. But, he kept his composure and inquired to Kenji on what dish it was he was to make.

"This is a snack from my home world," Kenji said, pulling a box out of his dimensional storage skill. "They are essentially thin cookies dipped in chocolate. However, we are having a difficult time recreating the cookies."

"And you would like me to try and replicate them?" Rory asked for confirmation.

"Exactly, feel free to try as many as you need to help you figure out the best recipe," Kenji said with a smile.

Rory took one of the treats and gave it a careful bite, all the while excited to be trying food from another world. The chocolate coating was unusually sweet, but it was indeed the cookie that seemed to hold some delicious secret. It was crisp and flakey, providing an almost nutty balance to the dish. The small round sticks packed so much flavor that Rory became extremely nervous about if he could indeed recreate it. All the same, he was ready to give it a try.

Rory took a bit of time to pace the kitchen, focussed solely on figuring out what mixture of seasonings would be best for recreating the flavor, as well as the cooking method that would provide the proper texture. He thought about asking Kenji for advice, but he was sure he could figure it out on his own. The chocolate coating on the cookie was also going to take a little experimenting, as the chocolate he was used to was far too bitter. Kenji, seeing how seriously Rory was taking this, waited patiently as he leaned against the door frame.

Just as Rory seemed ready to start his first attempt, Kenji straightened then excused himself. He had been called on by one of his spouses, and encouraged Rory to go ahead and begin his experiment. Before Rory could say anything in reply, Kenji was gone. Being left alone with the monster girl left him uneasy, but he decided to focus on the task at hand. Making a few different mixtures he first tried baking the cookie like center.

He worked meticulously mixing ingredients in different proportions in hopes of nailing the consistency. Try as he might to pour all his attention into his cooking, Rory could feel the eyes of the girl on him through every motion. As he continued to work, his focus moved more onto cooking. He had always been like this, when food was involved all else just faded away. It wasn't until he noticed the girl standing next to him that he froze in his tracks.

"You seem to be very good at this." The girl commented as Rory slowly returned to mixing a bowl of chocolate he had melted.

"I've dedicated my life to it," Rory dared to reply. "I may have been an adventurer for quite a few of my years, but I was taught to cook when I was still a child at home."

"So it's a life long passion?" The girl pressed.

"I guess so," Rory replied, turning just a little so she couldn't see his face.

"Then might I ask you another question?" The girl continued moving around to meet Rory's eyes.

Rory swallowed hard, but putting on his business smile gave her a nod to signal it was ok to ask her quandary. He immediately regretted doing this though as an eerie energy poured off of the girl. He felt his heart speed up and instinctually reached for a kitchen knife to protect himself. Before his hand could reach it though, she had placed her hand on top of his own. Putting barely any force into her actions she still managed to bring him to a halt.

"Why are you so nervous around me?" She asked leaning in so that only he could hear. "What do you think you could do to stop me?"

Rory kicked the kitchen counter and spun around, pointing the cleaver he had grabbed in the brief moment his hand was free. He pulled back his hand in preparation for the fight, but then the weapon was gone.

To be more accurate it was sticking out of the wall behind him. He looked the girl in the face, but he was surprised when there was no sign of blood lust.

"I don't think Lord Kenji would bring something harmful into the city," Rory said, deciding that maybe talking things out would be better for everyone. "But, I also know he is a kinder man than most. Should you pose a danger to him and the rest of the kingdom, I will not stay silent."

The girl chuckled to herself, then commented in an overly complicated manner that, "Should she ever turn down a darker path, it was nice to see the humans had people ready to stand against her."

"Then?" Rory questioned as the aura around the girl settled and to his eyes almost disappeared.

"Then nothing," The girl replied with a smile. "I have no intention of bringing harm to the people of this world, if I may be so bold I'd claim I am working for the benefit of the people. If you find me untrustworthy then please feel free to tell anyone you deem necessary of my nature."

"You're ok being labelled as a monster?" Rory asked, a bit puzzled. "Then I take it you aren't hiding yourself from Lord Kenji?"

"By the gods of old no." The girl said looking stupified. "Even if I had wanted to, he would easily have seen through me."

"He does seem rather observant," Rory agreed, nodding his head as he scratched his chin.

"Besides," the girl continued. "Kenji seems to think you can make my favorite snack, so I'll be sure to help protect you and yours."

"Is that really as deep as this goes?" Rory wondered aloud.

"Yep!" The girl responded, clapping her hands together.

Rory felt silly having worried so much over one of Kenji's companions. While he was glad to know his skills weren't so rusty that it was causing him to misjudge people, he felt nervous knowing a being this strong was so close to home.

"You needn't worry so much," The girl said, turning to walk back to her sitting spot on the counter. "I may be powerful but I'd never be so careless as to let others be caught in my crossfire. Believe it or not I'm older than I look."

"Then I guess I should call you LAdy from now on?" Rory asked the girl as he slowly returned to his food prep. The timer for the oven having just gone off.

"I prefer you call me Roxy," she replied.

"Roxy huh?" Rory commented as he pulled out the cookie sheet. "An alias I assume?"

"Very good," Roxy applauded him. "But that's enough questions for now."

Rory understood this was a statement not a suggestion, and as she seemed to be content with their exchange he continued his work. Dipping the cookies into the extra sweet chocolate mix he had prepared. Letting them sit so they could cool he turned to Roxy.

"I'll buy it for now," He said, extending his hand. "A friend of Lord Kenji is a friend of mine. Just know, I don't give many chances."

"Nor do I," Roxy said, returning the gesture.

About that time an apologetic Kenji popped back into the kitchen. He was a bit curious why his good meat cleaver was buried into a wall, but as no one was hurt or dead he decided he could get the details later. Instead he walked over to where the cookies dipped in chocolate had finished cooling.

Rory took one of each batch and handed them to Kenji and Roxy. They took a bite of each one, commenting on the closeness to the original and offering what advice they could. By the third try Rory had almost nailed the taste, and only the texture of the chocolate needed work. Rory was glad to see Kenji enjoying his food.

"Rory," Roxy said as she finished off the third attempt's leftovers. "Your talent is admirable. Might I be so bold to request your help with other confections of this nature?"

Rory was a bit flustered, having been called by name by this being and to have received a compliment on his craft. He scratched his head in an awkward fashion.

"If it pleases you, I'd be delighted."

Roxy smiled a toothy grin, then excused herself with the broken cookies that remained.

"You two have some kind of heart to heart?" Kenji asked as soon as Roxy was out of ear shot.

"Just a discussion on baking." Rory assured Kenji. "Now, how about I see if I can get the chocolate right?"

"Sure," Kenji said, patting Rory on the shoulder. "Let me know how I can help.

A Few hours later And Rory was on his way home. He still didn't know if he could trust Roxy, but at least he had satisfied her cravings. If nothing else in this world was true, it was that a full monster caused much less trouble than a hungry one.

Chapter 9

Toblin Marks, who was originally from the Ravnford Dutchie, found himself grateful he had participated in the trip to scout out land in Duke Simali's domain. After his dealings with the soon to be King, providing materials for one of his spouse's wedding dresses, his company had experienced insane growth. But, what he didn't expect, was to run into the young king to be while seeking space to expand his distribution network.

As Kenji walked up to the man, he seemed to have a minor heart attack at his changed appearance. However, with the grace of a thriving business man Toblin regained his composure in an instant. Recognizing that the Kenji before him was probably more influential now than he was in their previous meeting. Kenji extended his hand in greeting, and Toblin returned the gesture with a small bow.

"Now Sir Hero," Toblin started with a practiced smile. "What brings you to the Simali Dutchie? I had heard you were recently involved in a monster culling in the Capital."

"Indeed," Kenji replied, rubbing his head in an embarrassed manner. "I actually made the trip out here looking for some materials to use for armor. I've heard the wyverns in this area have incredible pelts, but you need permission from the Duke to hunt in his domain for them."

"Ah, I assume you have received permission then?" Toblin remarked a little disappointed he hadn't been able to offer up his services to Kenji again.

"Actually…" Kenji said with a slightly disappointed look crossing his face. "Duke Simali is sick at the moment and had to decline my visit for the day. So I've been instructed that I am allowed to purchase as much as I'd like but hunting them myself would require more time."

"Really!" Toblin exclaimed with maybe a tad too much excitement. "Ahem," he cleared his throat. "That is truly a shame as I'm sure you are more than capable of hunting the most vicious of the creatures. Though, if I may be so bold, I might have just what you're looking for."

"What?" Kenji said in shock. "Do you have access to good wyvern hides?"

"The best!" Toblin said, puffing out his chest with pride. "There is but a single problem with the materials I have in stock."

"Oh?" Kenji responded, raising an eyebrow. "I didn't expect you yourself to mention a problem with a product you were selling."

"I have pride as a merchant," Toblin remarked in a stern tone. "I take care to make sure only the best products are stocked by my shops, and in the event that something is not to the highest quality, I will never stoop to falsehoods about the goods."

"Much appreciated," Kenji said with a smile. "Then please tell me more about these products you have."

"Certainly, but let us go somewhere more appropriate." Toblin commented looking around for a nearby spot they could inhabit to conduct negotiations. " I have yet to open a store here in the Samali Dutchie , but I did make the connection to a hide procurer."

"Is it an adventurer?" Kenji questioned as he followed the man as he made his way toward a luxury inn near the city's center.

"Why yes," Toblin continued the conversation as he held the door open so Kenji could head inside first. "A young adventurer with splendid talent. He has reached B-rank at the age of 24."

"Interesting," Kenji spoke with an air of curiosity. "Please do me a favor and introduce me should the chance arise."

"It would be my pleasure." Toblin nodded as they approached a small meeting room on the inn's ground floor. "Please have a seat Sir Kenji, I'll have one of my men bring the goods to us in due time."

"Just Kenji is fine Mr. Toblin," Kenji responded as he took a seat in a slightly overstuffed sofa. "There is no need to be so formal with me in a setting like this. If I had it my way everyone would drop the formalities but my lovely spouse Mara has reprimanded me on being too casual in public settings."

"The Crown Princess is assuredly correct," Toblin said, crossing his arms in contemplation. "I can accept your request as we are in private, but to show a lack of respect to the future leader of Falist is a taboo for sure."

Kenji shook his head, having hoped that Toblin would just be casual with him in the future. But as they continued to chat for a while Toblin was sure to respect Kenji's request and treated him in a more familiar fashion. It wasn't till a knock on the door called their attention that he put back on his Professional tone and demeanor. A young girl brought in a chest that seemed several times too large for her to lift."

"This is my assistant for this trip," Toblin said, making a formal introduction. "This is Haylee Finet, I'm training her to be a full fledged merchant. I actually hope to have her lead the store I intend to establish here."

"A pleasure," Kenji said, extending his hand to the young woman. "My name is Kenji, an associate of Mr. Toblin."

The girl took his hand and shook it, with clear eyes she gazed up at him with a sense of awe. Kenji's eyes sent a flood of information to his mind, as he still wasn't used to controlling his upgraded eyes. In the flash however he could see that she was a member of the Demon race. Kenji must have made an odd expression as she gave a concerned glance at Toblin.

"My apologies," Kenji said as he released her hand. "I've never met a member of the Demon race."

Haylee went white as she took a step backwards. Toblin however was quick to take a step between her and Kenji. Toblin didn't think the man was the kind to judge people before getting to know them, but he really only had a gut feeling to rely on. On the off chance Kenji was one of the people who held the Demon race in contempt, he would not stand idly by. Even if it meant crossing the soon to be King.

"I'm so sorry," Kenji said bowing quickly. "I didn't know it was a secret, but I promise not to tell anyone if that will make up for my blunder."

Relaxing just a little, Toblin glanced back at Haylee. She seemed to still be panicking, but Toblin took a deep breath and nodded in understanding.

"We will be holding you to that, Sir Kenji." Toblin said with a gracious bow. "Haylee was the orphan of some visiting adventurers. I took her in as her father was a dear friend of mine. But ever since the contact with the Demon Continent of Helderon stopped, a large group of people led by a small faction of Nobels have started pointing to them as the cause of all our monster problems. It is a ridiculous notion, but I can't stop people from thinking what they will."

"I understand," Kenji said, seeming to grow more and more apologetic. "IT was never my intention to cause discomfort, but now that I have, allow me to apologize once more."

"It is fine," Toblin said reassuringly to Haylee.

"If you say so uncle," Haylee responded, still looking at Kenji with an air of mistrust.

Kenji, feeling desperate to set things right, opened his dimensional storage and pulled out an ornate box filled with chocolates. These were ones that Rory had made with the correct balance of sweetness to match those from Kenji's home world. Setting the container on the table he opened the foil on one of them and popped it in his mouth. Because it was a treat from this world his vampiric side didn't care much for it, but flavors had improved through his evolution. Gesturing for Toblin to try one as well, he reached out and placed one in a flustered Haylee's hand.

"What is this?" She questioned as Toblin began unwrapping a candy and inspecting it."

"I'll be," Toblin began. "Are these chocolates?"

"Indeed," Kenji said with a smile. "A friend of mine made them for me. I'd be honored if you'd try it."

Toblin flipped the disk of chocolate in his hands a few times, finding a deep appreciation for the smooth consistency. Then with reckless abandon he flipped it into his mouth. Haylee stared at her uncle as if expecting him to be poisoned. For a moment her fears seemed to be founded in reality as Toblin lowered his head so his face was obscured. But then, he tossed his head back as happy tears ran down his face.

"This flavor is devine," Toblin exclaimed. "I dare to say I've never had a finer confection."

Haylee swallowed hard as her uncle went to grab a second one of the treats. Cautiously she unwrapped her own candy, and she could indeed see the quality crafting of the sweet. Bringing it nervously to her mouth she took a small bite, and all the tension she had been holding slipped away in a second. The sweetness of the chocolate left her at a loss for words. But as she glanced over at Kenji who smiled at her sheepishly, she realized this was a sincere offering of apology.

"Sir Kenji," she said, not meeting his eyes directly. "I understand that you don't mean any harm, but please keep my secret."

"It is not my secret to tell," Kenji reassured her with a warmer smile. "Should you ever find yourself in trouble please reach out to me. I won't stand for someone resenting you simply for being born different."

Haylee felt tears creep into the corners of her eyes. But shaking her head she simply returned the smile and gave Kenji a small bow.

"It's ok to trust him," Toblin said as he patted her on the shoulder. "Now, let's get back to business."

Haylee nodded in understanding and pulled out a small key from her pocket. Inserting it into the lock on the chest she had brought in, she gave it a turn. The sound of a click signaling the opening of the box, Kenji leaned in closer to get a better look at the contents. Inside were pure white wyvern pelts, stored carefully so nothing would damage them. Kenji felt excitement in his chest as his special eyes told him the stats of this material. Their defensive abilities alone probably made it worth its weight in gold.

"I don't get it," Kenji began turning to Toblin. "What exactly is the defect of this product?"

"It has a few," Toblin responded with an inquisitive look at Kenji. "The first is its unbecoming color. No one wants armor that flashy in the middle of a forest or dungeon. It would draw the monsters straight to you. The second is its lack of affinity with any of the elements. It has no specific innate magical protection, and from a wyvern that is a huge drawback as they can't be enchanted to protect from magical damage. This is because of their low affinity with magic. The trade off being that it tends to not be strong against physical attacks"

Kenji thought it over for a moment, elbow in his left hand and his right on his chin. He understood that to the average mage or adventurer this would be quite the draw back. Enchanting for the most part enhanced a trait already relevant to the material and the less specific the base trait the less an enchantment would manifest. Red wyvern skin for example made excellent flame resistant armor. But Kenji was no ordinary adventurer or mage and he could see the secret to making these materials insanely strong.

"Is there anything else defective with it?" Kenji questioned as he seemed to be at an impasse with his internal debate to buy the material.

"Actually I still haven't told you the worst part," Toblin said pointing at the top piece of hide. "Try and pick it up."

Kenji was puzzled but obliged with Toblin's request. Reaching out he had a strange sensation pass through him. Like his body knew something he didn't as the momentum of his reach let his finger tips touch the hide. All of a sudden the magical energies that filled his body were sucked to and out of his fingers. Retracting his hand for half a second, Kenji felt as if he had a moment of clarity. Slamming his hand down on the material pile he felt an enormous amount of his mana being sucked into the stack.

"Sir Kenji!?" Toblin shouted out as he made a movement to free the young man from the merchandise.

In the next moment the pelts had turned a lovely silver color and the magic reaction seemed to end. As Kenji removed his hand the materials seemed to try to hold onto his skin. It was easily dislodged however, and it remained static in the chest after that. Toblin looked shaken, and poor Kaylee next to him seemed to bi in utter shock.

"You didn't pass out from mana exhaustion?" Toblin stammered out. "I didn't even know you could stay conscious if you full on touched the pelts. What in the Depths of Rena are you young man?"

Kenji turned and smiled at the two of them. He could see that this was unprecedented by the way the others were reacting, but Kenji couldn't help but feel he had procured a precious item.

"Toblin my good man," Kenji said, reaching into his dimensional storage and retrieving a large burlap sack. "I'll take the lot, personally endorse your store here in the

Simali Dutchie and provide an advance payment for you to hire adventurers to deliver as many white wyvern pelts to you as they can manage as quickly as possible."

"Sir Kenji," Toblin said in a confused manner. "What do you mean by endorsing my store personally? And why hunt more white wyvern?"

"I meant that I'd provide you with the capital to purchase or build your store front here in this Dutchie, you may proceed with my full backing for the foreseeable future. In addition, I will have Ridol prepare you a special position so that you won't have to get permission from the duke from now on to hunt wyverns. As to why I want the white ones..."

Kenji's eyes seemed to glow more than normal with his excitement. Toblin, sensing he wasn't going to get a straight answer about the hunting request, simply gave Kenji a small bow.

"I don't know how this will help you, but I swear to do my best to meet your expectations." Toblin said.

Kenji took the chest and placed it in his storage, then hefted the leather pouch that was about as round as Toblin was. The man nearly fell over from, what he could tell immediately was, a number of golden coins that could buy out the entire stock of his business three times over. It was one of his skills as a merchant to know something's monetary worth from within moments of handling it. As kenji turned he came face to face with Kaylee, and his eyes peered into her being. There he could see several fields of information, including her titles and class.

Kenji had to keep himself from lunging at her, a desire to confirm what he just saw flooding through his veins. As if sensing his restraint Kaylee took a step back, but Toblin weighed down with the money, could do nothing but watch as kenji gripped the girl by the shoulder. She looked pale as Kenji leaned in and asked her a question in her ear. She let out a startled gasp, but kenji could tell from the way her pulse quickened that she knew exactly what he had said. But then in a moment of contemplation, Kenji released her. Kaylee looked as if the life had been drained out of her.

"Sir Kenji," Toblin bellowed. "What was the meaning of…"

"Silence," Kenji said using his Commandment skill.

Toblin fell quite, literally unable to make a sound. Kenji looked at Kaylee and commanded her to tell him who she used to be. It was silent for a moment as the girl did her best to resist her orders. But slowly the magic overwhelmed her.

"Im Rachel Hearts, I was on my way home from school when I was hit by a truck and perished," her voice wobbled as she tried to keep more info from leaving her mouth. "Originally I lived… on a planet… called… "

Kenji held his breath as she tried to keep the last word from coming out.

"…Reighly…" she coughed out.

Kenji immediately dismissed his skills and Kaylee and Toblin were free to move once more. After that he got on his hands and knees and apologized to the young woman.

"I'm sorry I put you through that, but I felt desperate to know if you came from the same world I did."

"You're not from this world either?" Kaylee said then immediately clasped her hands over her mouth.

"Wow, way to keep your secret," Kenji said in a bemused tone. "I can erase Toblin's memory after this if I need to. But some time in the future, come tell me all about the place you came from. If possible I might be able to send you home eventually."

Kayle nearly fainted at the thought of getting to go home, Maybe a little too easily she started talking about things beyond

Kenji's Imagination. After she rambled for a bit and Toblin basically became a statue in the corner of the room, Kenji signaled for her to stop info dumping. Looking a bit embarrassed she took a step back and nodded.

"Need me to wipe his memory?" Kenji asked as Toblin wandered towards them, as if presenting himself to be caught unaware.

"Nah, Uncle Toblin is a good person. And now that I know a reincarnator can live a peaceful life here I'm glad."

"Very well," Kenji replied with a fangy grin. "Then until we meet again… Rachel."

The girl did a little swoon as kenji activated his teleportation skill and warped back to his estate.

Chapter 10

Upon his return to the estate, Kenji grabbed Reid from where she had been sitting with the others, and drug her off to her tower. They stayed locked in there, being brought food by Rinaldo a few times a day. It wasn't until a week later that Mara came to the research room and tentatively knocked at the door.

"Come in," an exhausted Reid called from within.

Mara cracked the door open, slightly nervous as to what they had been doing, and upon seeing the mess that filled the shop she seemed to almost think better of entering. But pushing on forward she hefted the door open to let some of the mid day light into the room.

The overwhelming scent of freshly cut wyvern hide hit her nose and she felt a little dizzy. Piering into the depths of the room she could see Reid laid across a work table.

"Are you alright?" Mara asked, approaching the worn out mage.

"Do I look alright?" Reid groaned from the table top, not sparing the energy to lift her head. "Your husband has had me working wyvern hyde and enchantment magic for days straight!"

"Speaking of," Mara continued as she patted Reid gently on the head. "Where is my husband?"

"Who knows?" Reid said, still unwilling to lift her head.

About that moment Kenji came rushing from behind a curtain, a pair of goggles strapped to his face that magnified his glowing eyes. In his left hand he held a needle with thread attached. In the other hand he was gripping a pair of very sharp looking scissors. Seeming to completely overlook his spouse for a second he went to get Reid's attention.

"Do we have any more magically reinforced thread?" Kenji asked in a hurried manner.

"Kenji," Mara said in a calm and clear tone.

Kenji snapped to attention, fully recognizing the presence of his beloved. He looked at her a little sheepishly as he quickly set down the tools in his hands so he could grab hers.

"Follow me," Kenji said excitedly, pulling her towards the curtain. "I've been working on something for the family."

Seeing how excited Kenji was, Mara made no attempt to resist him, following along where he led. Behind the curtain were a number of manikins. Each of which, upon closer inspection, had an outfit on it. As Kenji gestured for her to take a closer look, she approached a manikin that resembled her almost too much for comfort. The outfit on it was exceptionally beautiful with a white base and intricate needle work embroidering the edges and folds in a shinier white color.

"Well?" Kenji pressed obviously expecting some feedback.

Mara touched the clothes, and immediately felt her mana being drawn into it. As this occurred the base color turned an emerald green and the embroidered details shifted to purple. She took a step back in surprise and the cloth slowly faded back to the two tones of white it had started as. Glancing at Kenji she stepped closer and this time placed her full palm on the chest of the outfit. The same draining of MAna occurred and the vibrant colors shone with an increased warmth.

"I give," she said, turning to Kenji. "What have you done to make this fabric react to mana?"

"Nothing," Kenji said excitedly. It's all made out of the same material. I went and met with Toblin when I was in The Samali

Dutchie, and he sold me what he called a faulty product! Can you believe it?"

"What exactly was faulty about it?" Mara asked with an inquisitive look.

"The material is from white wyverns!" Kenji answered, and true to his hopes Mara seemed to recognize the unique trait of that variant of the creature.

"Those wyverns are nearly impervious to magic," Mara said, glancing back at the fabric. Reaching out she gave a firm tug to the sleeve, but surprising her nothing happened. Usually it would have torn under the slightest exerted efforts. "How did you do this?"

"I filled the material with enough mana to overcome the natural resistance that is inherent to it. With enough magic, the skin shifts to be suitable to the element most prominently present within the wearer. All of the fabric was silver when I first interacted with it, but by putting in just enough to keep it in a near full state, anyone who wears it with even the smallest bit of magic can take advantage of a wyvern's usual physical and magical protections." Kenji said, bouncing as he talked.

Mara had never seen him quite this excited over any of the other projects he had taken on in the past. It was rather cute, and she immediately started thinking of questions to keep him talking about his latest achievement. Of course, the first question was what he planned to do with the outfits he had made.

"Well," Kenji said, looking a bit starry eyed. "I will of course be giving these to the family, all those turned by my bite specifically. But assuming I've made them correctly, I will probably gift some to Gliph, Martha and Roxy. After that though…"

Kenji's words trailed off as it seemed a wave of exhaustion hit him. He took half a step forward, as if he was going to collapse to the floor, but Mara caught him in her arms.

"I may have gone a bit overboard." Kenji said with a smile up at his beloved.

"Lets get you and Reid back into the manor for a rest and a bath. After that's taken care of, you can tell me and the others all about your findings, sound good?"

"Sounds good," Kenji said, returning to his upright state, though only after giving Mara a quick kiss.

The three went back into the main residence, and after Kenji apologized to his four unhappy children, and two concerned looking spouses, he went and climbed into the bath. He hadn't realized how fervently he had been working, but if he was right these new armors made out of white wyvern skin could save many lives. But to find out how realistic his plans were, he would need to see how the prototypes performed. Still feeling excited he finished washing and made his way to the bedroom.

Zax was waiting for him, and as he entered the room they guided him to the bed. Sitting down they gestured for Kenji to lay his head on their lap. Kenji obliged and laid there peacefully while Zax messed with his hair. It was actually quite pleasant, and he quickly drifted into sleep.

— — —

The next day Kenji was fully recharged, and dying to have the family try out their new armour. Getting the other vampires from the castle, the full family gathered for the first time in ages. Reid was going to be working with Feni, JEnny and Wendy, while Kenji and his spouses would be their opposition. Kenji's group would be focussing on defence, having grown to be stronger than the others through their various evolutions. The others would be doing their best to land attacks as often as possible. And to the one who did the most damage to Kenji's team, there was a special reward.

Roxy served as an observer, having not been presented with new armour yet as Kenji was still working on a variation for hers. He didn't need to worry about adding his own magic to Roxy's, but he did want to make sure she was properly protected. Roxy didn't mind waiting, and even offered that she didn't need him to make her a special one. Kenji shook his head at her, and explained that regardless of her true identity, she was part of the family now. Touched by the sentiment, Roxy agreed she would wait excitedly for her own custom outfit.

The small mock battle took place at the knights' training ground at the castle. Ridol even made an appearance to see what the results were at Kenji's request. With everyone changed into their outfits, they each had unique appearances despite a standard masculine and feminine design option. The masculine one was more like a suit from Kenji's old world, with a mantle and flared pant legs for easier movement. The feminine version had knee high boots that met the hem of a long skirt with a slit in the side for mobility, as well as a snug fitting top and jacket that held their busts out of harm's way. The white materials definitely had been underwhelming at first glance, but as everyone took their set of clothing, they marveled at how they changed colors.

Feni's had turned yellow, a sign of her sensory magic that she excelled at. Jenny's became a warm orange, representing her affinity with martial magics. Meanwhile, Wendy's became Brown thanks to her strong earth affinity. The embroidered accents, a fun design that Kenji had chosen himself, looked like winding thorny vines that followed the edges and curves of the armour. They kept their white color as they didn't have enough mana to show their secondary attributes. Reid's however was a brilliant Icy blue with incredibly light red accents.

Mara looked fierce in her emerald green armour, with deep purple accents. Her overwhelming strength with wind magic and the burning mana within her dragon's core having dyed the outfit. Margret's was Crimson in color, with deep black accents as her blood magic was currently her strongest affinity, with her secondary abilities being based in strengthening magic. With that, all those wearing the feminine version were set to go.

Zax had opted for the masculine option as they thought it looked more epic. IT had immediately turned a charcoal black, a sign of her beastly strengthening magic, with Crimson accents as her vampiric nature shaded her natural mana. Finally, there was Kenji, Whose outfit remained almost unchanged except for a golden glow to his accents. The Light energy within him overriding the base attribute that the outfit could absorb. In all honesty, Kenji could be hit by a ballistic missile and probably come out of it without a smudge on his armour.

In reality, If Kenji wanted to, he could focus the rest of his mana into the material, and it would become stronger than any mythical defence spell. But it would require him to continuously release his magical energy, and even for him that limited the usefulness of the armour. It also made the material so rigid, he would have to stand in place and let attacks hit him just to make use of it.

The mock battle, now set to start, was the perfect chance to stress test Kenji's creations. In a moment, Roxy had signalled for the start and the opposing group lunged forward at Kenji's. The others were determined to put up a good fight against their comrades, knowing that this would be a different story if they were fighting back. Not moving from their positions, each of them allowed the others to get off their first attacks.

Kenji caught an Ice spear that Reid had produced in the chest, but did not budge from his spot. With a burst of energy he sent the projectile flying back at the mage, and it impacted her in the stomach. She slid back expecting to be taken out, but to her surprise she barely felt the impact. All the same, had it been returned at Kenji's full strength she thought she might have ended up with a hole through her.

Feni, who had disappeared so thoroughly that Zax completely missed her first strike, looked triumphant for a moment. That is till she heard the sound of her blade breaking against the specially designed outfit. Zax tilted their head to the side as they patted their side where Feni had struck.

"Good strength and form," Zax complimented her, "But let's see if you can take this!"

As Zax finished their statement they planted their foot in Feni's chest and sent her flying back. Once again the young woman seemed to come out of it unharmed, but with a broken weapon she was the first one out of the trial run. Jenny, who had always had an appreciation for the knights of the kingdom, picked Margret for her target. Channeling her strength into her sword she dashed forwards. She had been hunting monsters at the behest of the guild, and as such had duped a lot of skill points into getting abilities to better her combat abilities. One such skill was called severance, which allowed the user to cut through even metal with ease. But as her skill activated and her blade reached her target, her weapon also shattered.

Margret looked impressed, amazed that through self improvement Jenny had reached such heights. Even without blood magic, she could easily be considered beyond the S-rank adventurers that boasted supremacy in the guild. Unlike Zax, Margret just slammed her palm into the center of Janny's back, having slipped behind her after her sword broke.

Jenny stumbled forward and fell to the ground. She too was out of the test.

"Cant say how impressed I am," Margret commented, extending her hand to the girl.

"Thank you madam," Jenny replied, accepting the gesture.

Next, Wendy took hold of her battle axe and chunked it at full speed towards Mara. Mara, like the others, awaited the impact, but Wendy had other plans. She rushed Mara the moment the Axe was about to impact her, pulling a crossbow from her side. She thought if she got close enough she could put the princess in a position where she would have to surrender. The axe, however, clattered to the ground having done no damage. The moment Mara was free to move she waved her hands in a crossing motion that sent a blast of wind in Wendy's direction. The crossbow the only casualty of the interaction.

"You show promise considering your abilities were the least combat oriented of the three of you." Mara praised the woman.

"Oh darn," Wendy replied. "I thought I had…"

As Wendy tried to finish her statement everyone turned to see the massive fireball that Reid had summoned. Kenji was walking calmly towards her, but she seemed determined to beat him. Condensing the flaming sphere it shrank smaller and smaller as the flames went from red to blue. A trick that she had observed kenji using when he coated his weapons in fire magic. She wasn't sure if this would work, but it was worth a shot.

"Don't mind me," She said, feeling the extra eyes on her. "Just doing the best I can to destroy these silly costumes that took up the last week of my life!"

The attack flew at kenji as if it were tracking him, which Kenji assumed was part of Reid's plan. However he felt no need to run or deflect the attack, instead he turned his back to it. As it impacted him the flames burst forth as if to consume him. But the fire flowed over the armour as if it were water being diverted by a stone in a river. As the heat of the flames dissipated everyone stood in awe at the crater the explosion had dug out between Kenji and Reid, but past Kenji there was scarcely even a single patch of soil singed.

Kenji laughed as he turned back to see an obviously disappointed Reid. She had poured every last drop of mana she had into that attack, and while she knew kenji would be unharmed, she was annoyed the armour remained unblemished.

"That's it!" Roxy cried out. "The winner is team Kenji. Good show everyone."

Ridol stood and applauded the new Armour that Kenji had developed, and offered to help fund his continued research into the materials. Kenji thanked him but assured him that he had it covered for the time being. Kenji's work for the guild over the years had left him more than comfortably wealthy, and having never experienced that in his old world he was happy to spread his earnings around to his own endeavors. Ridol understood, and excused himself for his next meeting. leaving with Jasper who had arrived to fetch him.

Kenji gushed over his achievements, knowing while it might seem silly to some, that if his theory was right this armour could change the survivability of every adventurer on the continent and maybe even beyond. As the group walked towards the castle gate to return to their homes, Reid grabbed Kenji's arm.

"You promised!" She said looking him in the eye with a totally serious face.

"Yes, yes," Kenji chuckled in reply. "Rory's next experiment will be how to make ice cream. Are you satisfied with that?"

"Well duh," Reid snarked, but she couldn't hide the twinkle in her eyes.

"The kids will like that too," Mara chimed in.

"I want some as well," Zax shouted excitedly, raising her hand.

"I guess I could go for some," Margret interjected.

"I want chocolate flavored ice cream," Roxy added .

Kenji laughed once more, and felt a happiness that left him in an amazing mood. But, it did make him think a little. There was still so much to do. A world to save, Monsters to beat, gods to find and an evil to be stopped. It seemed he still had a long way to go to truly save the world of Rena. Looking at his family though he was certain that they were capable of making this place as safe as it could be. If kenji could, he would make sure everything turned out alright. Here where he lived with his loved ones, where he was chaperone to a god and protector of the peace. All this because he had died during the hero summoning and was now a Demi-god.

Made in the USA
Coppell, TX
15 February 2026

71360198R00132